Charles W. Marshall

Celebration of the One Hundred and Fiftieth Annibersary

Anatiposi

Charles W. Marshall

Celebration of the One Hundred and Fiftieth Annibersary

Reprint of the original, first published in 1871.

1st Edition 2023 | ISBN: 978-3-38212-612-4

Anatiposi Verlag is an imprint of Outlook Verlagsgesellschaft mbH.

Verlag (Publisher): Outlook Verlag GmbH, Zeilweg 44, 60439 Frankfurt, Deutschland
Vertretungsberechtigt (Authorized to represent): E. Roepke, Zeilweg 44, 60439 Frankfurt, Deutschland
Druck (Print): Books on Demand GmbH, In de Tarpen 42, 22848 Norderstedt, Deutschland

CELEBRATION

OF THE

One Hundred and Fiftieth Anniversary

OF THE ORGANIZATION OF THE

TOWN OF LEICESTER,

JULY 4, 1871.

CAMBRIDGE:

PRESS OF JOHN WILSON AND SON.

1871.

PROCEEDINGS.

In accordance with a previous public invitation, the citizens of Leicester held a meeting at the Town House, February 11, 1871, to consider the subject of celebrating their One Hundred and Fiftieth Anniversary in some suitable manner; and after discussing the matter it was voted to do so, and a Committee was chosen to invite an Orator, and other preliminary measures were taken to carry out that object.

Meetings were subsequently held at various times; and it was decided that the day of our National Anniversary was the most suitable and convenient time for this purpose.

On the 20th of May, the citizens were again called together to organize for the occasion, and

> JOHN E. RUSSELL, Esq., was chosen *Chairman*, and
> Dea. C. C. DENNY, *Secretary*.

A Committee of Nomination was appointed, who reported the following names, which were accepted, as a

Committee of Arrangements.

JOHN E. RUSSELL.	L. S. WATSON.	L. D. THURSTON.
JOHN D. COGSWELL.	JOS. A. DENNY.	JOHN S. SMITH.
C. C. DENNY.	L. G. STURTEVANT.	D. E. MERRIAM.
WM. F. HOLMAN.	CHARLES A. DENNY.	EDWARD SARGENT.
JOSEPH MURDOCK.	A. H. COOLIDGE.	JOHN WOODCOCK.
SAMUEL MAY.	ALONZO WHITE.	JOSHUA MURDOCK.
EDWIN L. WATSON.	LUCIUS M. WAITE.	ERVING SPRAGUE.
CHARLES SIBLEY.	JOHN N. MURDOCK.	LUCIUS WOODCOCK.

Cheney Hatch.	John W. Bisco.	William P. White.
Charles W. Warren.	John N. Grout.	Dexter Knight.
H. Arthur White.	James Whittemore.	John D. Clark.
Samuel Firth.	Samuel L. Hodges.	Lyman I. Upham.
Josephus Woodcock.	Jos. M. Trask.	D. W. Kent.
T. E. Woodcock.	H. O. Smith.	Samuel Southgate.
James A. Smith.	Billings Mann.	Albert Marshall.
Anthony Hankey.	Thos. S. Livermore.	William Bond.
Parley Holman.	E. G. Carlton.	Arthur M. Stone.
Rufus Holman.	Dwight Bisco.	Joseph B. Upham.
George H. Munroe.		

At a subsequent meeting Messrs. RUSSELL and DENNY were made permanent Chairman and Secretary of the Committee of Arrangements ; and the whole Board were divided into various Sub-committees to carry out the details of the Celebration.

Weekly meetings were held for some time previous to the Fourth of July, to report progress in the work, and provide for its satisfactory completion.

The following general invitation to the Absent Sons and Daughters of Leicester appeared in the daily and weekly papers in Worcester; and five or six hundred copies, in the form of circular letters, were sent out by mail, by the Committee on Invitations, to those whose address could be readily ascertained : —

SEMI-CENTENNIAL CELEBRATION AT LEICESTER.

The citizens of Leicester will celebrate the ensuing Fourth of July, in Commemoration of the One Hundred and Fiftieth Anniversary of the Organization of the Town, by an Address from Hon. EMORY WASHBURN, and other appropriate exercises.

A Dinner will be provided at as low a price as can be afforded, not exceeding $1.50 a plate.

The present citizens of Leicester, together with Spencer, Paxton, and Auburn, a part of which territory was originally included in Leicester, and all the Sons and Daughters of Leicester now scattered abroad, are cordially invited to unite with us on this occasion, without a more particular invitation.

All persons intending to be present are respectfully invited to communicate with either of the subscribers, on or before the twentieth day of June, giving information of the number of Dinner tickets wanted, and provision will be made for all who thus apply.

By order of the Committee of Arrangements.

JOS. A. DENNY, }
L. D. THURSTON, } *Sub-committee.*
CHARLES A. DENNY, }

LEICESTER, May 31, 1871.

As the day approached, all things seemed to be made ready for the occasion.

Committees had reported that Hon. EMORY WASHBURN, the Historian of Leicester, had been invited, and had consented to deliver the Address ; that all needful arrangements for music, instrumental and vocal, had been made ; that AUGUSTUS MARRS, of Worcester, had engaged to provide a dinner for about one thousand persons ; that a large tent from Boston had been engaged, to be erected on the common in front of the Town House, and tables set for over one thousand plates therein ; and that a suitable place had been prepared in the grove in front of the Academy for the Orator and his audience.

Officers of the day were chosen as follows : —

JOS. A. DENNY, Esq., *President.*

Hon. WALDO FLINT, of Boston, ABRAHAM FIRTH, Esq., of Boston, Rev. SAMUEL MAY, L. S. WATSON, Esq., JOHN WOODCOCK, Esq., and S. L. HODGES, Esq., *Vice-Presidents.*

Capt. JOHN D. COGSWELL, *Chief Marshal.*

Dr. JOHN N. MURDOCK, *Toast Master.*

The morning of the Fourth was ushered in, as usual on our National Anniversary, by the firing of cannon and the ringing of bells ; and Leicester Hill was made cheerful by the early arrival of friends from abroad, who continued to throng to the village during the early hours of the day.

The weather, though cloudy and somewhat threatening for a while in the morning, proved to be fine and wholly favorable throughout the day. The exercises in the grove commenced at ten o'clock A.M., and were in accordance with the printed programme.

Rev. SAMUEL MAY said, that in the universally regretted absence of Mr. Russell, the duty of acting as Chairman of the Committee of Arrangements, had been assigned to him. In behalf of the Committee, and of all the citizens, he congratulated the large audience on the happy circumstances of the occasion, rejoicing especially to see so great a number of former residents returning to take part in its memories and festivities. At his call, the WORCESTER NATIONAL BAND, which had already been filling the village with the echoes of its awakening strains, opened the exercises with a suitable piece.

Mr. MAY. — One of our own poets has said, —

"The groves were God's first temples;"

and in such a temple, fair to see, and, as we can truly say, "not made with hands," are we met to observe our country's great anniversary, to recall the struggles, sufferings, and virtues of those who first planted this town, and to render honor to their character and their work.

The whole audience, led by a well-trained choir of thirty singers, then sang, to the tune of Old Hundred, the following

INVOCATION.

Great God, to thee we raise our prayer,
Our grateful song for thy kind care
And guiding hand, which all our way
Has led us, till this gladsome day.

Here on our nation's natal day,
Here 'mid our fathers' graves, we pray
That we their virtues may possess,
Their courage, faith, and holiness.

Rev. A. H. COOLIDGE, Chaplain of the day, read the following passage of Scripture : —

"Give ear, O my people, to my law : incline your ears to the words of my mouth.

"I will open my mouth in a parable : I will utter dark sayings of old :

"Which we have heard and known, and our fathers have told us.

"We will not hide them from their children, showing to the generation to come the praises of the LORD, and his strength, and his wonderful works that he hath done.

"For he established a testimony in Jacob, and appointed a law in Israel, which he commanded our fathers, that they should make them known to their children :

"That the generation to come might know them, even the children which should be born ; who should arise and declare them to their children :

"That they might set their hope in God, and not forget the works of God, but keep his commandments."

After which Mr. COOLIDGE offered a fervent, appropriate, and impressive prayer.

The choir next sang the following original Hymn, written for the occasion, by Rev. A. C. DENISON, of Middlefield, Conn., a former Pastor of the First Congregational Church of this town : —

> From far and near to-day we come,
> As children to our early home,
> These pleasant scenes again to greet,
> These friends of by-gone years to meet.
>
> These smiling vales, these massive hills,
> These gleaming lakes, these laughing rills,
> Are little changed from year to year ;
> Ah ! not so we who gather here !
>
> But where are they who dwelt upon
> These hills in seventeen twenty-one ?
> Life's busy walks no more they tread,
> Their names long numbered with the dead.
>
> It may be we shall never more
> Clasp hands upon this earthly shore ;
> But may we, an unbroken band,
> All meet at last at God's right hand !

Following which the band played "Keller's American Hymn."

Mr. MAY said, — To most of this audience the Orator of the day needs no introduction. A son of Leicester, he has always loved his native town, and given her many sure proofs of his affection. We recognize him as the conscientious and able lawyer, the learned jurist and just judge, and a Governor of our State. But here and to-day we more gratefully honor him as the Historian of Leicester, diligent and faithful. To that history we have summoned him to make to-day a further contribution; and we are all here to listen to the Hon. EMORY WASHBURN.

ADDRESS BY EMORY WASHBURN.

LET us congratulate ourselves, my friends, that, on a day dedicated to the commemoration of a nation's independence, we are permitted to gather once more around the altar of a common home, and live again in the pleasant memories which cluster around this consecrated spot. Let us congratulate ourselves that it is our privilege, at the close of a hundred and fifty years from the organization of our native town, to read, in the prosperity which greets us on every side, how wisely its founders planted here the germinal principle of a free and independent community, in the solitude of the wilderness and upon the then verge of civilization.

In the light of its history, and of that of the little band who first made a lodgment here, we may read an epitome of the agencies which, upon a broader field, built up a colony into a State, and spread out the little belt of population that then hugged the shores of the Atlantic into a vast and mighty republic.

But, interesting as this might be to any generous mind, there is a deeper sensibility awakened in some of us on revisiting these pleasant scenes. Busy Memory repeoples it with the forms of loved ones; and the friends of earlier days that used to meet us in these familiar walks start up, in fancy, at every turn, to welcome us back to our former homes. Households long since scattered are thus gathered once more around the hearthstone where they played in their childhood. But, as we pause till a sense of what is real comes back upon us, we find that —

> "Our playmates have passed on,
> And left us counting on the spot
> The faces that are gone."

There are, mingled with these emotions, lessons of deep philosophy to be drawn from such a commemoration as this. The busy world stops for a day, and gives us a chance to look back over the way along which our fathers and we have been travelling, and to measure the progress which, as individuals and as a community, we have been making in this lapse of years.

Counting by the annual recurrence of the seasons, the present completes the hundred and fiftieth since the people of Leicester were organized into a town. The first meeting of its inhabitants for the transaction of municipal business appears to have been held on the first Monday of March, 1721. The propriety of commemorating this event was obvious; and those having the matter in charge wisely concluded to unite with it the celebration of the declaration of our national independence. And it only needs a single suggestion to impress upon every one the fitness of such a union. The one event was the birth of a town, the other the proclaiming of the birth of a nation; and the relation between the two becomes more apparent as we trace the connection there was between the action of the towns of New England and the achievement of the independence of the nation.

The real causes and origin of the American Revolution lie far back of 1776. The spirit that gave it life, and animated the counsels which guided the Colonies in their struggle with the mother country, may be traced to the Puritans of Old England, but took its most active and efficient form in New England, in the little independent democracies, called towns, into which the Colonies of Plymouth and Massachusetts Bay were early divided.

The country has been so long familiar with this division

of territory into separate townships, that we are apt to overlook its influence and importance. But I doubt if any one thing has done so much towards promoting and sustaining their capacity for self-government, as a people, as the organization of these little democracies. In this consists the great difference there is between the people of the old world and our own. In France, for instance, every thing emanates from a central power, and the government takes care of the internal and domestic affairs of the people in their cities and villages. The police is ever present to protect the citizens, and enforce the laws. And when, therefore, they undertake to proclaim a republic, they fail, because, instead of governing themselves from within, they are so accustomed to an outside force to regulate them, that they fall into discord and confusion, till some strong hand seizes hold of the administration and restores order by substituting a single will for the combined wills of the nation. Whereas, from the very first, the people of New England have been accustomed to manage their own domestic affairs by the free and intelligent action of the citizens in their town-meetings, and were so far independent of any general government over the whole, that when its administration in Massachusetts was suspended from Oct. 5, 1774, to July 20, 1775, the towns went on conducting their own affairs in quiet and order, and, in fact, supplying a government for the whole province, till it was again organized under the advice of the Continental Congress. Nor does it speak well for the maintenance of the democratic form of government which was sustained by the self-regulating power of the towns, that, instead of exercising their own police, they have been made dependent, for the most important department of it, upon men appointed by the executive of the State. Such was not the theory or practical working of the system which laid the foundation of these self-regulated republics in New England. While as colonies they recognized the sovereignty of the home government, they were, as to their domestic affairs, as free and independent as we are to-day. The freemen of Massachusetts came together in their own towns upon terms of equality of rights, where every one had a voice and a vote. They chose their own local officers, selected their ministers, regulated their schools, voted their own moneys, and saw to their disbursement. As parts of the larger body politic of the colony or province, they chose each its own delegates to meet in a common assembly to make the general laws by which they were to be governed. And so important did they deem this coming together of the representatives of the several towns in what, from the first, was called the General Court, that the occasion became a general holiday of the people, which, under the name of Election Day, came down from the planting of the colony till some of us were old enough to enjoy the well-remembered sports and amusements to which it was devoted.

It was in this way that the colonists not only learned how to govern themselves, but how to take care of themselves. And in doing this, it was the towns which spoke and acted, and their action became the pulse and tone of the sentiment of the colony. In the absence of newspapers, the town-meetings became the medium by which the people examined and discussed the political questions of the day; and the doings and resolves of Boston were echoed back from every town in the country. Among the instances to which I might allude, where the people came together in their respective localities to consider the great questions in which the country was interested, and where a sentiment was matured upon which the people as a nation ultimately acted, was that of this town on the 26th May, 1776, upon the subject of declaring the Colonies independent of the British Crown. On that day the people of Leicester were called upon to consider this momentous question. They came together, and by a solemn vote, without a dissenting voice, pledged themselves, " that in case the Honorable the Continental Congress should declare these Colonies independent of Great Britain, they would support said Congress in effectuating such measure, at the risk of their lives and their fortunes." And this was followed in June by a like resolve by the people of Spencer. And nobly did these towns redeem that pledge, though it is altogether beyond my limits, on this occasion, to dwell upon the details of the part they took in achieving that independence. There is, then, I repeat, a fitness in thus uniting the commemoration of the two events to which this day has been consecrated.

But, in doing this, we are to remember that the men of the Revolution were not of the generation who planted the town. More than fifty years had intervened between these events; and, if we would do justice to the actors in both, we must go back, and call up before us the men and women who were the pioneers in penetrating this, till then, unbroken wilderness. Who and what manner of men they were who laid here the foundation of a community which at the end of a hundred and fifty years are sharing the fruits of their faith and their fortitude, is a theme worthy of such an occasion.

In the first place, they were of pure English stock. Several of the families were direct immigrants from England, and none of them were more than two or three removes from native English parents. With scarce an exception, they were small farmers, who did their own work, and relied upon their own resources. There must, in this way, have grown up a condition of great equality among them, while their isolation from the rest of the world, which rendered them mutually dependent upon each other in many things, must have bound them together by strong ties of sympathy and attachment. The growth of the town was slow; and the families of which it was composed were scattered over its entire territory, so that there was nothing like a village or group of dwellings within it for many years. It could have had but few attractions, at first, to draw new settlers to it. They were in constant fear of the Indians, and had to build " garrison houses " in different parts of the town, to which they could flee when threatened with attack. There is a letter on record which was addressed by some of the most consi brable men of the town to Lieutenant-Governor Dummer, in 1725, which gives us some insight into their condition. " It was so late," say they, " the last summer, before we had any soldiers, that we were exceedingly behind in our business." And in another they tell him that this is a frontier town, and has been much exposed, and reduced to very low circumstances, by reason of the late Indian wars. The town, moreover, was so poor that the province abated that year's tax which had been assessed upon it.

What is said of its being a frontier settlement was literally true. There had been one in Brookfield; but it had been broken up and dispersed by the Indians during Philip's war, and only a few families had begun again to establish themselves there. With this exception, there were no white settlers between Leicester and the Connecticut River. On the east a few families had gathered in Worcester, after the destruction of that settlement, in the same year with the one at Brookfield. Even with those settlements there was next to no means of communication. The only pretence for a road was a path through the woods, which it was difficult to travel even on horseback. It was along what was called the "Connecticut Path," by which persons going from Boston to Connecticut River threaded their way through the wilderness. It had never been laid out as a highway until after the organization of the town; and, when that was done, it took the name of the "Country road," which was the same, substantially, as that which was travelled here fifty years ago. The roads to the north and south from the present village were commenced at a still later period; so that, when the people of the town took upon themselves the burdens and responsibilities of supporting the civil and religious institutions of a body politic, they were an isolated community, dependent upon themselves alone for success. By a wise foresight, there were reserved, from the grant of the township, a lot of land for the ministry, and another for a school. But as no provision was made for a house for public worship, the people came together and erected one in 1719, two years before they had been organized as a town.

But before we inquire how far they redeemed the pledges they made to the colony and posterity when they assumed to act for themselves, it would be pleasant to gratify a natural curiosity which every one must feel to know something more of the character and condition of the men who laid the foundation of a social structure which has stood firm amidst all the changes through which the country has been passing. In this connection, too, we are inclined to ask, What were their aims and purposes in coming here, and under whose patronage did they come? Unfortunately, they left no record of themselves, save here and there an isolated fact, from which, however, we are able to infer what that record would have been if it had been preserved. Of some things connected with their history, we can be at no loss for a judgment. And, in the first place, they recognized no man as master or as patron. They came in the consciousness of their own integrity, to build up homes here, and to share the civil and religious privileges of a respectable New England town. Within that happy mediocrity of life for which Agur, in his wisdom, prayed, they had "neither poverty nor riches," and seem to have been content with that humble lot. Rich and poor are, indeed, relative terms; and I have sought for some test by which to judge how far these words were applicable to the first settlers of the town. I have accordingly looked into the inventories of the estates of several of them, which were made up at different times, from fifteen to forty years after the first settlement of the town. The real estate of Judge Menzies, which was one of the largest in the town, although incumbered with mortgages, was valued at £2,700, and his personal at £319. John Lynde, Jr., a still richer man, and perhaps the richest of the original settlers, had lands valued at £1,377, and personal estate of the value of £900. Of those estates forming something like an average with others in the town, I find the amounts varying from £327 to £680. But while these statistics help to show the pecuniary condition of the first generation, there are other facts to be collected from them which throw further light upon the condition and habits of their domestic life, which are equally curious and interesting. Thus, for instance, while these inventories are very minute and particular, even to trifling articles of furniture, I have found neither carpet nor clock nor watch in any one of them; and while we can imagine that they would have substituted, as they used to do, sand for carpets, and a scratch on the window-sill for a clock, to tell them at what time to eat their dinners, it is difficult to conjecture how they contrived to live without looking-glasses. The men must have worn their beards as long and shaggy as some do in our day, without ever thinking of a razor; and as for our mothers, it was lucky for their toilets that no evil genius had before that day invented that strange outrig for the brain, a *chignon*, or discovered how to pile a bale of dry goods upon a woman's back and call it a lady's dress. In the inventory of the richest man in town, I find three of those necessaries of life, looking-glasses, varying in value from 6*s*. 9*d*. to 40*s*. In that of another man of substance, I find only one of the value of 4*s*.; while among the household goods of others no article of the kind is to be found. But the most curious contrast with the habits of our day is found in the matter of books. In many a well-to-do family we do not find a single volume. John Lynde, Jr., whom I have already mentioned, was the first school-master in the town, and held the office of justice of the peace, when it was really a mark of distinction. He had what is called in his inventory a " library of Latin books and English," which was valued at £1 16*s*. 3*d*.; while the books of three other substantial farmers varied in value from 5*s*. to 15*s*. Such as had any books generally possessed a Bible; and we occasionally find a psalter and a psalm-book. But the use of psalm-books was rendered unnecessary by the universal custom of the deacon in leading the singing in public worship, reading a single line of the psalm at a time, which was taken up by the congregation, and repeated by them in chorus rather than in harmony.

Perhaps I shall have no fitter place in which to speak further of the social habits and domestic lives of the good Puritan fathers and mothers who flourished here a century and a half ago. As we look back upon what we know to have been their surroundings, as well as upon the lives of incessant toil and self-denial to which they were subjected, it would seem to be a misapplication of terms to speak of their pleasures or amusements. Every thing they saw and heard must have checked every approach to joyousness and hilarity. In the day-time their vision was hemmed in by the tangled forest, into which the sunlight hardly found its way. Their slumbers at night were broken by the howling of wild beasts around their dwellings; while within, sickness was often a dreaded visitor, and death every now and then stole in upon their scanty number, to snatch from them the companion they could least spare. What could there be in such a life but sadness and sorrow, and the constant foreboding of coming evil? But, fortunately for them as for us all, there is a silver lining to the darkest cloud, and a light that relieves the most sombre picture. Human nature has an element of joyousness in the young, the hopeful, and the contented, wherever they are found; nor was it wanting even here. That their pleasures partook of what we are taught to call gayety or fashionable life, is not to be imagined. Such a profane thing as dancing must have been unheard of. Dress and style furnished rather a narrow range for fashion, where the goodwife spun and wove and dyed the cloths which she afterwards cut and made into garments for the family. They doubtless had their social gatherings, and the tattle and gossip which made up the talk of every neighborhood. But they had never reached the luxury of a "tea-party," for the reason that that delightful beverage first began to be heard of in the colony in 1720. They had to manufacture their own news, as there were only two small weekly newspapers then printed in the province; and as they had neither post, nor mail, nor stage-coach, these probably never found their way so far into the country. But, where there are youth and health, nature is not niggard of its elements of pleasure. There was hunting in the forest and fishing in the streams. The young men had their matches of strength and agility, and the old men told to willing listeners, the stories of English life and what the Puritans had suffered. And so life moved on. The young people came together and loved and courted and married, and started in life with the same rose-colored hopes that they do now, though, in their simplicity, they had never thought of turning a wedding into a "gift enterprise," by taxing the bounty of every guest they invited. Children were born to gladden the household, as they do now; and in the rearing and training of these, parents were too busy to feel the want of frivolous amusements. Even toil and labor put on the garb of pleasure and social enjoyment, when neighbors came together to help raise each other's buildings, or by the light of the golden harvest moon sat and husked one another's corn, or crowned the achievement of a new co-operative bedquilt by an evening of free and cheerful hilarity. In these and a hundred other ways the kindlier feelings within them found room for free play, and pleasures sprung up as spontaneously as the wild flowers and fruits around them which ministered to their senses.

But we must look deeper than these outside forms of social life for the efficient causes of the traits of character which we discover in these early settlers. There were a variety of circumstances which were calculated to foster within them habits of thought which made them self-reliant and independent in sentiment and opinion. In the first place, there was a practical equality in their social and political condition, which contributed to their individual independence. In the next place, a large proportion of them had been born in Massachusetts, and had imbibed in their childhood the prevailing notions of Puritan belief and independent church polity which the Congregational churches of New England had adopted. Many of them, doubtless, had been more or less trained in the common schools of the colony, and had learned the important lesson of self-government in the town-meetings in which they had taken a part. Another circumstance which ought not to be overlooked was that they owned the lands which they tilled, and were no man's tenants. It is difficult for us, with our habits, to realize the practical difference there is, in point of manliness and independence of spirit, between owning lands and occupying them as tenants. One sees it everywhere in England ; and in France the old system of feudalism, which kept the great body of the cultivators in the condition of slaves, was never broken down till the Revolution of 1789, — more than a hundred and fifty years after the farmers of New England had been accustomed to till their own lands and to think their own thoughts.

The scattered and isolated condition of the early settlers of the town left them much alone, and drove them to habits of self-reflection and self-examination. If they knew little of the outer world and what we call science, they were conversant with the workings of their own hearts, and dwelt much upon the solemn and mysterious connection there is between man and his Maker, in the light of that revelation which they accepted without reserve. Darwin's wonderful discovery of man's relation to the ape had not disturbed their confidence in the Bible account of the creation of our first parents. The vaunted philosophy of Positivism had not then got in advance of revelation, as we are now told it has done. Nor had modern theorizers found out a better code of moral law than that which our fathers innocently believed was delivered on Mount Sinai. And while it would be out of place to raise questions of creeds on such an occasion, it is not to be denied, that the Calvinism of that day was calculated to make a class of profound thinkers, whatever may be thought of its doctrines as a system of faith. The very effort to comprehend and reconcile with one's reason the inexplicable mysteries of original sin, of free-will and fore-ordination, was an exercise of intellectual gymnastics which helped to develop and strengthen powers of the mind which, under ordinary circumstances, would have been likely to lie dormant and inactive. Right or wrong, it was just such a system of faith as was suited to fit that generation for the work which they were commissioned to do. That they were religious men of the then prevailing school of theology is seen in every step of their growth and progress. Sunday was to them a day of sacred rest; and their children, trained in the mysteries of the Shorter Catechism, grew up in the nurture and admonition of the Lord.

Another circumstance which showed the character and spirit of the men of that day was the manner in which they struggled against their pecuniary embarrassments in their attempts to establish and maintain a free school. In 1731 they made provision for such a school, but were obliged to suspend it the following year, though they resumed it in 1733. Nor were they able to provide a school-house till 1736, when they built one of the humble dimensions of twenty by sixteen feet, and six feet and an half " between joints." This, moreover, was the only school-house which the town had for many years, and stood upon the Common, a few rods to the east of the meeting-house, of which I have already spoken.

Passing from the social and intellectual condition of the people to the circumstances in which they must have found themselves in respect to the number, size, and situation of their dwelling-houses : as near as can be ascertained, when they built their meeting-house, it was placed in the woods upon the common land, and only two houses had then been built near it, — one where Mr. May's now is, the other where Captain Knight's stands. The latter was of a single story, kept as a public house, and was furnished with wooden hinges and latches which were raised by strings passing through the door. And in this respect the same was doubtless true of every house in town. I have a description of what is now the village from an eye-witness who knew it in 1767, fifty years after the first settlement of the town. The public house which I have spoken of had just been burned ; the little nondescript school-house was still standing; a rude brush fence, which came up to the meeting-house at its rear, inclosed the burying-ground then in use. The dwelling-house of the first minister stood some fifty or sixty rods to the north-east from the meeting-house ; and a small building, containing two rooms, stood where the tavern now is. If to these we add a small house near the brook, west of the Common, and another between that and the Common, a small house upon the slope of the hill east of the meeting-house, and two or three small houses upon the south road (one of them near where the late Mr. Hobart lived), we have the entire village and its surroundings as they were within the memory of persons who have described them to some of us who are here to-day. And I may perhaps add, in respect to the style of the buildings of that day, that the house now standing on the east side of the road, half a mile north of the meeting-house, was, I imagine, one of the most imposing structures in the town, and none of these were at any time painted.

If now we attempt to gather hints from the meagre records before us to guide us in our study into the characteristic qualities of the men and women who left their impression upon the society which they planted here, our only regret is that we are so circumscribed in our inquiries. If, as we are told, " the child is parent of the man," the first settlers of a town are not only the physical parents of the future generations of that town, but give to their moral qualities a shape and

character as distinctly marked as the complexion or personal
habits which distinguish families from each other. Applying
this test, I am led to believe that, with all the counteracting
influences which tended to make them selfish and exclusive, they
had an element of liberality in their natures which amounted
at times to magnanimity. Their convictions in the matter of
religious belief must have been strong and decided. They
took upon themselves a heavy burden when they undertook to
maintain the stated ordinances of the gospel, and must have
felt it almost as a personal wrong if one of their number broke
away from the communion which had bound them together.
It must have, therefore, been a severe trial of their spirit of
forbearance, when, in 1736, before the troubles in which they
had been involved in their long controversy with their first
clergyman had been healed, Dr. Green gathered, in what is
now Greenville, a society of Anabaptists, and became himself
their preacher. And yet I cannot find that this secession
brought with it any of the accustomed alienation of feeling
between those who composed the two societies. But this, perhaps, should excite no surprise after we are told that the town
had already safely passed through a far more severe invasion
of the Orthodox proprieties of church order in 1732, when Ralf
Earle and seven others certified to the town-clerk, who, though
an excellent tailor, was an indifferent model for good spelling,
that they were what he chose to record them, " those people
called Quackers," which was followed a few years after by
Steward Southgate leaving Mr. Goddard's church, and joining
these recusant seceders. What makes it the more remarkable
is, that all this took place while the memory was still fresh of
what the colonists had done to convince these two classes of
religionists of the error of their ways, by hanging a few and
banishing more. They were too dull to accept the force of
the argument, and kept on multiplying worse than before.

But, from some cause which I am ready to believe was good
sense as well as liberal sentiment, the fathers of this town
seem to have early reached a conclusion to which half the
world is still slow to yield, that a man may be a good neighbor
and a valuable citizen, though he may differ from the majority

in matters of speculative theology. And this sentiment they seem to have transmitted to their children ; for when a colony of Jewish families removed here from Newport, during the war of the Revolution, they not only found a ready welcome, but intimacies and friendships grew up between the citizens and them, which lasted as long as they lived. The town and parish remained entire until 1833 ; and the fact that the pastorates of six ministers cover the whole hundred and fifty years shows the general harmony which has prevailed upon subjects upon which people are so apt to betray feeling and ill-blood. To understand the force of this, we ought to remember how great have been the changes in a denominational point of view within the memory of persons now living. I had grown almost to manhood before I ever saw what I supposed was a Catholic in the town ; and one or two would, I think, have covered the entire number of Methodists ; and as for Unitarians, the term had then hardly become known here. Whereas now the regret is, not that each of these denominations and Episcopalians have a place of worship here, but that the religious society which was the first to secede from the original parish lives here no longer, save in its honorable history, and the memory it has left of the worth and intelligence of those who commanded for it the respect of the entire town.

While we may well honor the catholic spirit which seems to have characterized the place, we ought to remember how much of this harmony has been due to one who for fifty-nine years has been the guide and pastor of the church which was founded with the town itself. His influence has been felt in the prosperity as well as harmony of the town, and has added value to every farm and workshop and manufactory within it. Posterity will honor his memory, as those who have met him in his daily walks have honored him.

Let it not be supposed, however, that while dwelling upon the old-fashioned ways and notions which had so much to do with the character of the earlier and later generations of the people here, I have been unmindful of the progress which the race has everywhere been making, nor how far the world, through the progress of science, has got in advance of many of the superstitions which kept down the free action of the human mind. I have no time to dwell upon the assumed triumphs of modern science over the credulity of a former age. But we cannot, in passing, forbear asking ourselves which of all its discoveries could have supplied our fathers, for an hour, with the support they found, in their periods of gloom and discouragement, in the evidences they saw around them of a present God, and the unquestioning confidence with which they read in their Bibles the sublime truths which in their simplicity they believed he had himself revealed to man.

There is another characteristic incident in the lives of these men, which is the more remarkable, when we remember that they were mere farmers' sons, whose unromantic habits of life were associated with home and the quiet, unexciting pursuits of peace ; and that is the readiness with which they yielded to the calls which were so often repeated for men to take part in the military enterprises of the day. I know not how many of its citizens went into the service in obedience to these calls : but wherever I have been able to trace the history of the expeditions in the "French wars," as they were called, I have found the names of Leicester men upon their rolls. They were at the taking of Louisburg in 1745, where Captain Brown commanded a company. They were in the Canada expedition in 1747, and with General Winslow in that to Maine in 1754. They were with General Abercrombie at Crown Point in 1756, and with General Amherst at Ticonderoga in 1759, in both of which William Henshaw was a lieutenant. And more than thirty officers and soldiers from the town took part in the conquest of Canada in 1760. Indeed, so many had taken a share in these wars, that some of us can remember with what familiarity the older men of the town used to speak of the events of these campaigns, which made the names of Crown Point and "Old Ti" almost household words among the people of that day.

And it may be to this cause that we should ascribe that traditional respect for military titles which once prevailed so universally here and throughout New England, and of which we may now see traces in the prefixes attached to so many names which are inscribed on the older head-stones in our cemeteries. They were marks of distinction which had been won by gallantry and desert in fields of actual service, and were cherished and respected accordingly.

It was by these "old French" wars, as they were called, that the men of New England were trained in the school of the soldier for the coming struggle for our national independence. And nothing, in all its stirring and memorable events, was more fraught with hopeful interest to those who were watching its progress than the manner in which seemingly raw troops, gathered from the farms and villages of the country, without organization or discipline, or even knowing who was their commanding officer, stood in an unbroken line, and received the fire of the advancing columns of an enemy whom they were meeting for the first time, until they could deliver a fire in return, with so sure and steady an aim that the finest troops of England quailed before it, and fell back with a recoil from which it was difficult to rally them. Leicester and Spencer had their men there too; and when the company made up of these were ordered by the commandant of the regiment to which it belonged to halt at Charlestown Neck, which they reached after the battle had begun, they to a man refused to obey the order, and gallantly followed their captain, who led them into the thickest of the fight, and they were among the last in the retreat.[1] Nor did this martial spirit of its men flag for a moment, till their independence had been achieved. In addition to those who marched at the alarm of Lexington, and those who enlisted in the first eight months' service, and in addition to more than thirty who served in the regular Continental army, the town answered, during the first five years of the war, twenty-eight drafts for men, although the entire number in the town capable of bearing arms, in the year 1781, was only one hundred and fifty-one. With such a history before me, I looked with no little solicitude for the record of what Leicester had done during that last grand struggle for the Constitution and the cause of human liberty against a wicked

---

[1] The captain was Seth Washburn, of Leicester; the lieutenant, Joseph Livermore, of Spencer.

and groundless Rebellion ; and I only wish I could give it entire, as it has been given to me. I quote when I say, "Her sons marched at the first call of the President for the defence of the capital, and were among the first armed troops to reach Washington. They received their first baptism of fire in the streets of Baltimore, with the old Sixth Massachusetts Regiment, April 19, 1861; Colonel Jones, its commander, and others among its officers, being natives of Leicester." She sent into the service more than three hundred of her sons. They were in more than one hundred battles. More than forty of them were wounded, and twenty-one of them fell on the bloody field. It was the story of the Revolution over again. It was the Leicester of the fathers revived in the action of the sons.[1]

In what I have thus far said of the character and intelligence of the settlers of Leicester and their immediate posterity, as well as of the part they took in the events of the Revolution, I ought, perhaps, to have spoken more at large of the individuals who, from education and position, exerted an influence upon the conduct and opinions of others. While I should be unable to name, much less to do justice to, all who deserve notice, I have ventured to mention a few of these rather as representatives of the period in which they lived, than from any wish to signalize any, where so many are equally deserving. Among them Judge Menzies stands the earliest in point of time. He had been bred as a Scotch barrister, and held the office of Judge of Admiralty in the province, which was one of much dignity and importance, and brought him into contact with those engaged in foreign trade, as well as the men of influence in the province. His estate was what is now known as the "Henshaw place;" and he could hardly have failed to exert an influence over his neighbors by the style in which he lived, and the example which he set before them, socially as well as personally, in his manners and address.

Of the earliest native-born children of the town, I have in my mind two, whom I name in connection with the problem how that generation could have acquired the education which

---

[1] See Appendix.

is now supplied by our schools. But that they were well educated by some means, is apparent from the history of the town, as well as the recollection of some still alive. Thomas Denny was born three years after the town was organized; and his sister, Mrs. Nathan Sargent, three years after that. This was some years before any school had been established; and the distance at which they lived from it must have rendered it of little or no use to them when it was in operation. And yet there are those living who remember this lady as a person of agreeable culture and great intelligence; and it would be difficult to name one who could better represent the patriotism of the women of the Revolution, who were not a whit behind their brothers in spirit or devotion. It was of her that the incident has so often been told, how when the company of minute-men, of whom her son was one, were on their march for Lexington, on the alarm of 19th April, 1775, they halted at her door, but not being supplied with bullets for their cartridges, she and her husband took the leaden weights from their clock and melted them down, to supply the want. It told more than words could do that war had indeed begun in earnest. The brother, Mr. Denny, would have been a leading man in any community by his intelligence, patriotism, and public spirit. He died just before the breaking out of the war; and his loss was felt as a public calamity in the province. While a member of the General Court, he was associated with such men as Samuel Adams, James Otis, and John Hancock, and is named by Governor Hutchinson in his History. He had taken a part in the celebrated controversy with the Governor in 1771, which was one of the immediately exciting causes of the Revolution.

Two of her citizens, Colonel William Henshaw and the Hon. Joseph Allen, by their relation to the leading men of that day in Boston, formed an important medium by which the spirit of Adams and Otis and Warren was widely diffused through this community. Mr. Allen was a nephew of Samuel Adams, and removed here in 1771, and did much, by way of his pen and his personal influence, to give a right direction to the sentiment which animated the people. Colonel Henshaw was in the cause from the first. He was the Adjutant-General of

4

the American army until the arrival of General Washington at Cambridge, and acted in that capacity for some months after. He was of the Council of War, and recommended the occupation of Bunker Hill, which led to the battle of the 17th June. He was afterwards lieutenant-colonel in the Continental service, and fought in some of the severest engagements during the war. He was long a type of that courtesy which distinguished the gentlemen who had been trained in the military school of the Revolution. But, in attempting to speak of individuals, I should at once be at a loss where to stop, if it were only to name the men and women who in their several spheres did their full share towards building up the town and sustaining the country in its struggle. I should have to speak of the farmers who contributed of their hard and scanty earnings to keep the church and the school from being closed, as was done in other of the towns, caring for the soldiers' families in their absence, and going in turn themselves when needed, to fill the ranks of the army. I should have to tell of the wives and mothers, who, with more than Grecian or Roman heroism, went on training up their children in the ideas of the true dignity of manhood, and supplying by their own lessons of wisdom and experience the teachings of the schools, and inspiring within their sons a desire for that learning which their own limited opportunities had denied to them in their youth. If I have any claims to the place with which you have honored me to-day, I owe it to the lessons of a mother, who, coming from a neighboring town, had never enjoyed the advantages of a school beyond a single week. A history of those days would show that the mothers and daughters were as much in earnest as the sons and the fathers. And, living as we do in an age of progress, the thought starts up, in spite of the gravity of the hour, how, after having brought up their children to honorable lives and generous purposes, the mothers of that age went down to their graves in blissful ignorance that they had been all their days cheated out of their rights, in never having voted at the hustings, or made a speech at a caucus; though, if it would not be turned against us in the coming contest, we ought in frankness to confess that the country would have been quite as well off, if the ballots of half the men who did vote had been written for them by their disfranchised sisters who were denied the privilege.

In speaking of the causes which have helped to give a character to the town, we ought not to forget the influence which the Academy has exerted in educating the successive generations who have come upon the stage since it was founded in 1783. Nor should we ever cease to honor the memories of Colonels Crafts and Davis, who were its founders, nor of those who, from time to time, have been its patrons and benefactors.

But while the town, from the causes to which I have referred, was able to sustain an honorable rank as an orderly and intelligent community, there were causes at work adverse to its material growth and advancement. Its soil was hard and unsuited to profitable agriculture. It was remote from market, and its isolated situation had little to attract new settlers. I well remember the man whom I knew in early life, who " rode post," as it was called, during the Revolution, between Boston and New York, and carried the public letters and despatches between those cities. As the journey had to be made on horseback, it took an entire fortnight to go and return. The first stage-coach between Boston and New York was established in 1783, and the town was without any post-office until 1798. For these and other causes the growth of the town was exceedingly slow. Its territory originally embraced a portion of Paxton and Auburn ; but, including these, for the first forty years after its settlement there had been added less than one hundred families. During the period of the Revolution it made no increase, and in 1790 it had added only seventy-one to what its population was when that war began. And even if we come down to 1820, although the State, exclusive of Maine, had since 1776 increased more than eighty per cent, Leicester, between those periods, had added but two hundred and forty-seven, or less than twenty-five per cent. In the mean time she had been sending out her sons and daughters to help people Vermont, Maine, New York, Ohio, and Virginia ; and wherever they went, they carried with them the habits of thrift, enterprise, and good order in which they had been trained in the homes in which they had been reared.

Fortunately for the town, while this had been going on, an element of prosperity and growth had been developed which has since turned the tide of its prosperity, and scattered evidences of thrift on every side, although we look in vain for many of the farms on which some of the best families who flourished here in our childhood were reared and educated. The manufacture of cards had been begun here soon after the Revolution; but that of woollen cloths was inaugurated in 1814, by one whom, at the ripe age of eighty-nine years, we welcome here to-day as the pioneer in that great source of the prosperity which we witness in the villages which have been springing up here by the magic power of mechanical enterprise and ingenuity.

Never has there been a more signal illustration of the value of home industry, or of the wisdom of encouraging home manufactures, than is here exhibited in the changes through which the town has been passing during the life of a single individual. Art has literally triumphed over nature, and turned the once fitful brooks, which ran to waste between drought and freshet, into perennial sources of enterprise and wealth.

If we were to contrast the population and wealth of the town at the date of my own birth with what we now find it, we should be told that the eleven hundred and three inhabitants of that day had multiplied to twenty-seven hundred and sixty-eight; and the valuation, as returned by the town, of $182,000, had grown to that of $2,000,000.[1] Nor is there any secret as to the manner in which this change has been wrought, when we read in the Statistics of the Industry of Massachusetts for 1865, that the woollen goods and cards manufactured here in a single year exceeded in value $1,600,000, employing a capital

---

[1] The statement here made requires a word of explanation, lest a wrong conclusion should be drawn in undertaking to compare the valuation of the town in 1800 with that of 1870. The statement as to 1800 is taken from Mr. Felt's work on the Statistics of the State, collected from authentic sources. I am led, however, to conclude that the valuation, as returned for purposes of taxation, must have been below the actual value of the property of the town, for I find in the assessment of the United States direct tax in 1799 the houses and lands liable to be assessed in the town were valued at $238,869. Either can probably be little more than an approximation to the true value.

of half a million, and the services of almost half as many persons as there were people in the whole town at the close of the Revolution. Political economists may speculate about the fancied benefits which are to flow from free trade. Here we have a living proof around us of the blessings which have actually flowed from a wise protection of home industry.

Style and manner of living, in the mean time, may have changed, and the frugal habits of the fathers may have given place to what would have seemed to them an unwonted display of luxury and extravagance. But there is nothing in this for apprehension or alarm, so long as the elements of character which made them what they were, are cherished and respected by those who are filling their places in the social structure which they built up here. All will be safe, if, as the passing generations look back upon the institutions which their fathers planted, and the example of true manliness which they illustrated, the sons shall emulate their virtues, and imitate the courage with which they always stood by the right.

If there is danger from any cause, it is that a generation shall arise, who, secure in the enjoyment of what their fathers earned by diligence, frugality, and prudence, shall forget that the true dignity of a people is not in the magnitude of their wealth, or the splendor and style in which they live. There is a dignity of manhood which outweighs them all, and in the loss of which a nation is bankrupt, though rolling in wealth and luxury.

> " Ill fares the land, to hastening ills a prey,
> Where wealth accumulates, and men decay."

And on such an occasion as this we can hardly forbear to muse and meditate upon what is to be the future of this our early, our honored home. Who is bold enough to read in the simple annals of its past history a forecast of the next hundred years ? Is the progress of the last to be an earnest to the next century of its growth and prosperity ? Less than a century ago it took nearly as many days to reach New York or Albany as it now does hours ; while we read in papers of the morning the events which transpired yesterday in Paris and

San Francisco. Science, too, in all its multiform departments, has been making such wonderful progress, that the child of to-day knows a thousand of its profoundest mysteries, which puzzled and confounded the wisest philosophers of that day. And when I remind you that we ourselves have witnessed the invention of railroads and telegraphs, and have seen pain and suffering disarmed of its terrors by the still more signal discovery, by Dr. Morton, of the anæsthetic power of Ether, who will dare even to guess what a single century is to bring forth?

To us as individuals the question is of but little moment. But as parts of that endless current of human life which is to flow on when another generation shall have taken our places, every generous heart yearns to have the mystery solved, not for a single town alone, but for this vast and mighty continent, whose boundless domain had hardly been opened to the tread of the white man when our fathers chose this spot for a home. The imagination is lost in conjecture as it vainly attempts to sketch in outline a picture of what they are to witness who are to stand where we do at the recurrence of another jubilee. But may we not rest assured that when that day shall come, it will find, all over the continent, the ripened fruits of that germ of civil liberty which was first planted here in Massachusetts, and to maintain which her sons helped proclaim and establish a nation's independence, which we have met to commemorate? May we not glory in the thought that before that day shall come, even the old world will have started into new life under the example of what we are witnessing, and that the tinsel and glitter of rank and royalty will have grown dim in the light of the noble dignity of a universally free and enlightened manhood?

We have come here to-day, my friends, to gather lessons of wisdom from the simple annals of the fathers who on this spot filled their spheres of duty with honor and fidelity. We have come here to call up the memories of the past, and to wipe away the moss and dust which have been gathering over the names of loved ones, which affection had carved upon the head-stones that mark where they are sleeping. We have come to spend one more day amidst scenes and associations over which memory sheds a soothing and a holy calm.

To-morrow we shall again join the busy throng, and mingle in the bustling activities of an anxious world ; and a new century will take up its record, to be read when another jubilee shall again call back the sons of Leicester to the homes of their fathers. With some of us that record is soon to close. But the mind will, again and again, recall the memories which this day has awakened, till, one after another, we shall all have joined that procession which has been passing off this stage ever since our fathers planted on this spot the institutions of civil liberty and Christian civilization, a hundred and fifty years ago.

APPENDIX.

LEICESTER IN THE LATE WAR.

THERE were representatives of Leicester in nearly every regiment that left Massachusetts during the war, also in many regiments out of the State and in the United States navy and regular army.

Her sons marched at the first call of the President for the defence of the capital, and were the first armed troops to reach Washington. They received their first baptism of fire in the streets of Baltimore with the old Sixth Massachusetts Regiment, April 19, 1861; Col. Jones, its commander, and others among its officers and men, being natives of Leicester; — were next under fire at Big Bethel and Ball's Bluff; — many of them participated in the Burnside expedition to North Carolina; — were the first men to land on Roanoke Island, commence the battle, and the first to enter the rebel batteries there; — were the first men to enter the battle of Newbern, and also the first to break the rebel line and enter their fortifications. They were in nine regular battles in North Carolina; and one held an important command on one of the gunboats, which, under Admiral Goldsboro, swept the rebel fleet from the waters in North Carolina.

Again in Virginia, they were with McClellan in all his Peninsular campaign, from Yorktown to Malvern Hill; — with Pope at second Bull Run and Chantilly, at South Mountain and Antietam again with McClellan, with Burnside at Fredericksburg, with Hooker at Chancellorsville, and with Mead at Gettysburg, experiencing with the Army of the Potomac its varied fortunes.

Leicester had her representatives at the taking of Forts Walker and Beauregard on the South Carolina coast, at the siege of Fort Sumter, at the blockade of Wilmington and Charleston, at the taking of Fort Pulaski, Ga., Forts Macon and Fisher, N. C., with Farragut in the passage of the forts at the mouth of the Mississippi (on the frigate Pensacola), also with him in his great naval battle in Mobile Bay.

In the West, a Leicester boy was in the battle of Mill Spring, and witnessed the fall of the rebel General Zollicoffer, was at Pittsburg Landing, Tenn., and Corinth, Miss.; — had several representatives with Rosecrans at Perrysville, Stone River, and other battles; — with Grant at Chattanooga, — one of his batteries, which helped break the rebel centre on Mission Ridge, was commanded by a Leicester boy, — also at Franklin and Nashville under Thomas, with Banks at Port Hudson, and with Williams in his heroic defence of Baton Rouge.

They were with Sheridan in all the hard fighting in the valley of the Shenandoah, at Fisher's Hill and Winchester battles, and other battles there; — went with Grant from the Wilderness to Richmond, in many of the battles at the siege of Richmond and Petersburg, to the surrender of Lee; after that marched with Schofield to join Sherman " coming up from the sea," and after the battle of Wise's Forks joined him in his last blow at armed Rebellion in the South.[1]

There were something over three hundred men in all, and the names of over one hundred regular battles in which Leicester boys participated can be given. By land and sea they always did their duty nobly and well. We know the names of twenty-one killed in battle or died of wounds, of nine who died of disease while in the service, besides many who died after their return in consequence of exposure and hardship while there.

Upwards of forty were wounded, and we know of five who starved to death in Andersonville, Milan, and other rebel prisons.

These facts speak for themselves.

---

[1] A son of Leicester parents commanded an Ohio Regiment in Sherman's march " to the sea."

Hon. EMORY WASHBURN.

DEAR SIR, — The above items in regard to the Leicester soldiers I gather from the soldiers' records and from personal knowledge. If you can make use of them and any other information in my reach, it will be given cheerfully.   Very truly yours,

H. ARTHUR WHITE.

The address occupied somewhat over an hour in delivery; it was pronounced in a full, clear, and strong voice; and it was readily heard by the large audience in the grove, and from the neighboring houses. The attention given to it was noticeably close, and continued to the end, when warm and cordial applause gave sign of the general pleasure.

The band gave a further and varied performance; at the close of which a benediction was pronounced.

The Chairman then introduced to the assembly the Chief Marshal of the day, Captain JOHN D. COGSWELL, who gave notice of an intermission of half an hour, at the close of which the procession would be formed, in accordance with an order which he announced.

Punctually at half past twelve o'clock the procession was formed upon the Common, the right in front of the Town Hall, marched around the Common, and filed, section by section, each under direction of its special Aid, into the spacious tent, whose white and swaying canvas was an ornament to the village. There, at the ample and bountifully furnished tables, over eight hundred of the sons and daughters of Leicester, native and adopted, were quickly seated; and a more cheerful company, or one more fair to look upon, it were not easy to find. A blessing was craved by the Rev. Mr. COOLIDGE, Chaplain of the day; after which the attention paid to the various courses, from fowl to fruit and ice-cream, was as unremitting and assiduous as the high temperature of the weather would permit. A short breathing spell, during which the band played " Hail Columbia," intervened between the last course and

THE SENTIMENTS AND RESPONSES.

Joseph A. Denny, Esq., as President of the day, opened the feast of reason and wit, by the following speech of welcome : —

Fellow-citizens and Friends, — We have met this day on an interesting occasion, to enjoy together a few hours of social intercourse. We are happy to greet so many of our friends and former fellow-citizens, who have in times past gone out from us for fields of greater usefulness. We are happy to bring to mind our earlier days, and to contemplate together the virtues of our ancestors. We have been led back to-day to those times, now far beyond the memory of any of us, when our ancestors planted their homes on these wild and rocky hills, subdued the wilderness, put in operation those moral forces, and established those civil institutions which have been to us so great a blessing. We welcome you now to this festive board, to the homes of your fathers, to our own hearth-stones, and to our hearts. We shall be excused, if on such an occasion, after contemplating as we have done the early history of our town, we express somewhat strongly our honest pride in this review, not only in relation to its first settlers and its Revolutionary history, but with its character and standing down to the present time. Our fathers exerted an important and salutary influence in the councils of the Commonwealth and the nation, in the organization of the State and general governments ; and since that time we have sent out from our homes many of our choicest sons, who have filled stations of importance in various departments of public life, up to the highest civil offices in our Commonwealth. We have sent forth our share of soldiers to fight the battles of our country in all her wars, and have furnished many of the higher grades of military officers, who have honored themselves and their country by their skill and bravery. Our sons have been found in the Cabinet of our nation, and in various departments of our general government, — in the executive chair of our good old Commonwealth, as judges of the bench and lawyers at the bar, as mayors of our large cities, as presidents of our important banking institutions, as managers of our vast railway corporations, as skilful physicians, surgeons, and mechanics, and successful bankers, brokers, merchants, and manufacturers, thus taking the lead in the business affairs of our growing country. You have often heard of the noble Roman matron presenting her children as her choicest treasure, exclaiming, " *These* are my jewels ; " and with a like pride in our common family, we this day honor our noble ancestors by pointing to their descendants, who derived from them their habits of industry, their stern integrity, and all the other qualities which go to make up the successful business man, the good citizen, and the patriotic statesman. " Here they are: look at them."

We trust that the occasion which has brought you together will cement more firmly the friendship of the citizens of this and the neighboring towns, whose common origin leads them to honor the same worthy ancestry, and to increase, if possible, the love of our absent sons and daughters for their early homes, our affection for them, and our interest in their future prosperity and welfare. Not because you have been prodigal in wasting your substance in *riotous living*, but because you have been prodigal in dispensing to the world around you the blessings which you have inherited from your ancestors, we have this day killed for you the fatted calf, and called you back to the homes of your fathers ; and again, in the name of the citizens of old Leicester, I bid you all a cordial welcome.

At the close he introduced the Toast-master, Dr. JOHN N. MURDOCK, who gave as the first sentiment, —

1. " *The Scattered Children of Leicester.* Though our narrow boundaries afford not scope for the energies nursed in their blood, and they, true sons of the Pilgrims, must themselves be pilgrims, and ' sing the Lord's song in strange lands ;' wherever their lot may be cast, may they be true to the traditions of their race, and always turn with yearning hearts towards home."

The PRESIDENT remarked, — I am happy to know that there is a large number of friends present who could with propriety be called upon to respond to this sentiment, but I see one near me whose family have taken a prominent part in the business of the town for nearly a century past, who was himself born here and spent his youth and active life in our midst, filled many town offices, and ably represented us in both houses of our State Legislature, but who has for many years past been prominent in the management of the financial affairs of our State capital, — and called on Hon. WALDO FLINT, of Boston, who said : —

He supposed he had been called upon to respond to the toast just read, on the presumption that he could not have lived so long without having learned something which might interest, for the moment, the large audience before him. He was not disposed to deny his age, inasmuch as, in that neighborhood, it could easily be proved against him ; nor did he deny that the supposed presumption, as a general rule, was fairly deducible from the fact of his age; and yet, as everybody knows, circumstances alter cases. Some live long and learn very little, — at least, little that is worth talking about ; others, who have really treasured up something of what they have seen and heard, have not the happy faculty of telling what they know in an agreeable manner ; and then, again, memory is exceedingly capricious in its moods, sometimes refusing to give out what is wanted until the occasion for using it has gone by, and then volunteering to give the information when nobody wants it. His own memory, he supposed, might be an average one, but in no respect equal to that of his friend who had so felicitously instructed and entertained them in the forenoon. For himself, he must confess that he remembered nothing which happened before he was born ; but were his friend just referred to, who had so diligently studied the history of the town from its foundation, to be quietly " interviewed," it would be no matter of surprise to any one who knew the loving interest he takes in the subject, to hear him claim that he was personally acquainted, more or less intimately, with most of the original settlers. The speaker's memory ran fairly back into the last century. One event near its close (he was not sure about any thing earlier), an event which spread a deep gloom over the whole land, he certainly remembered, — the death of Washington; but even that might have gone into the receptacle of things forgotten, but for the simple fact that he, and all the other children who attended Aunt Hannah's school, wore a badge of mourning on the left arm.

"The scattered children of Leicester!" *Scattered*, indeed! for there was not, probably, a State or Territory in the Union where some of them were not to be found. Could his hearers, and especially those in middle life, take in, readily, the full meaning of the word? Could they easily realize the marvellous changes which had taken place, not since this small municipality was organized a hundred and fifty years ago, but only during the present century? Seventy years ago the boundaries of the United States were Maine and Georgia, the Atlantic and the Mississippi; though even then that great river of the West was, to most persons, little more than a myth, — a small French settlement at New Orleans, a military post or two on its upper waters, to look after the Indians, visited by a few wandering trappers, and that was about all: almost as little known as when La Salle floated down its current in his little canoe, a hundred and twenty years before. A large part of Pennsylvania and New York, and the whole of the territory north-west of the Ohio, was an almost unbroken wilderness. Less than seventy years ago a young man and his wife concluded to remove from Leicester to what was then called the Black River country, in Northern New York, not far from Sacket's Harbor. The enterprise was considered so bold and daring that it was for weeks the principal topic of conversation at every fireside in the town. New England was then the East. Some twenty years ago the speaker met a young gentleman from Wisconsin, and asked him whether he had ever been East before. "Oh, yes, sir," he replied; "I have been to Ohio several times." What was now the East he did not know. The present boundaries of the United States were the Atlantic and Pacific, Oregon (saying nothing of our recent purchase

from Russia), and the Gulf of Mexico. What will they be
when the children come up here to celebrate their next jubilee,
fifty years hence? Who can tell? Speaking for himself alone,
he would say that, inasmuch as there were now good natural
boundaries on the east and west, and a fair chance for expan-
sion latitudinally, he was inclined to believe that neither Europe nor Asia would be annexed before that time; but further
he would not venture to express an opinion.

The toast expresses the hope that her scattered children may
ever retain a kindly regard for the place of their birth. He had
no commission to speak for others; many were present to answer for themselves; but he had no doubt what their answer
would be. For himself, he would say that he loved the dear
old town from the bottom of his heart. He could apply to it
in all sincerity the words of the sweetest of English poets, —

> " Where'er I roam, whatever lands I see,
> My heart, untravell'd, fondly turns to thee."

How could it be otherwise? Where does the sun rise in such
glory, or set in such a flood of splendor? And where has any
wanderer from the fold ever found a more health-inspiring atmosphere than upon his own native hills? Indeed, it had been
said that the old law of life — " threescore and ten " — was
overruled in Leicester, and that few died there under the age
of ninety. But the charm for him was not, solely nor mainly,
in external nature. It was something more closely intwined
round the heart. He could not help associating with the place,
nor fail to remember with the deepest gratitude, the parents
now sleeping in yonder graveyard, who watched over his childhood and youth with the tenderest care and love; nor could he
ever forget the acts of kindness and the words of encouragement which he received from all the inhabitants of the little
village, men and women, old and young, and which made his
early life one long summer day of enjoyment; nor could he
forget the many friends, still living, who, as often as he visited
his native home, greeted his coming with a most cordial welcome. He would be glad to present sketches of some of his

early friends, long since passed away; but he was already trespassing on time which belonged to others, and he must close.

The growth of the town had been very slow. In 1765, when the first State census was taken, the population was 770. In 1865 it was 2,527, — an increase of only 225 per cent in a hundred years, or only 17½ a year. The increase, however, in material wealth, and in the comforts of life, had been much greater. This slow growth (he was free to confess it) suited his old-fashioned notions; it argued firmness and stability, and was in harmony with the character of its inhabitants. They had never been a fast-going people, but still always making headway, though sometimes obliged to beat up against wind and tide.

He begged leave, in conclusion, to propose a toast which he thought would meet the approval of the older, and he hoped would give no offence to the younger, portion of the audience.

" *The Prosperity of my Native Town.* May it be in the future what it has ever been in the past, — sure, though slow."

2. " *The Old Leicester and the New.* On both sides of the sea."

The PRESIDENT said that in all the preceding remarks of the day, we had only gone back to the organization of this town; but we were ready for any emergency, and he was happy to introduce a gentleman to respond to this sentiment who was *old enough* to have been born in *Old* Leicester of *Old* England, and who early in life came to this town, was an honored and respected citizen for many years, was one of the " fathers " of the town, and faithfully represented us in the State Legislature. He had now for many years acted a prominent part in the management of one of our great railroad corporations, and he hoped that he and the directors of the Boston and Albany Railroad Company who were present would live long enough to improve their road by bringing it where it ought first to have been built, passing very near this and the centre village of Spencer. He called upon ABRAHAM FIRTH, Esq., of Boston, who said, —

MR. PRESIDENT AND DEAR FRIENDS, — I have abundant reasons to remember gratefully this town. Your kind introduction, sir, and this generous welcome, are in harmony with all the past. I was always treated as one of your kith and kin. The name of Leicester is near my heart for all this, and also because it is that of the city of my birth on the other side of the sea.

But before I go further, let me thank the Committee of Arrangements and whoever first suggested this gathering. There are generous men, you know, who decry giving prominence to places, and who advocate a cosmopolitanism which would indeed almost put them beyond our remembrance or serious thought; but I am of those who believe, undoubtingly, that he who is the best son, brother, husband, and father, the best lover of his native or adopted town, state, and nation, is the very best citizen of the world; and that these relations prepare the way, and are the indispensable steps to the larger citizenship.

And but for the committee, we should not have had, on this charming day, the pleasure of the many meetings of long-tried and, in so many cases, long-separated friends; nor the retrospect of the past honorable history of this town, by one of the ablest and most loyal of her sons, to which we have all listened with so much delight to-day.

Your toast speaks of the old and new. To the child, yesterday is old; but the higher and broader the culture of the mature man, the farther away is the old, and the contrasts of time are but the shifting scenes in one great drama, while

> " To THEE ! there's nothing old appears :
> Great God ! there's nothing new."

But the old, on this occasion, refers to our personal recollections and experiences in this town. Mine go back forty-four years, or nearly one-third of the time since the town had a municipal organization.

I remember the drinking habits of that time vividly. The country store in the east village kept an open bar, and no thought of shame attached to it. Strong liquors were offered on all social occasions; at weddings and funerals; drunkenness was common; and the general opinion was that all efforts to change these ancient customs were fanatical and absurd. Experience was on their side, and all experience was against the new reform. I remember Dr. Nelson, then in his prime, happily yet spared to witness, although not to participate in these services, I remember his coming into the school-house, and telling us the time had come to abstain wholly. Scoffs and jeers passed idly by him. I honored him then, and have honored him ever since for the kind, pious, and brave way in which he delivered the truth on this subject. And there came with him " Addison " Denny to circulate the pledge. All thanks and honor to him for that. To-day he is our honored President.

You know, sir, it is sometimes said that the temperance efforts of the past did little permanent good; but every one whose memory runs back no farther than mine, and contrasts that time with the present, knows better. But don't let me deny there were fanatics. Why, sir, how rare it was and is to find a man whose reason is so clear that he always maintains a true poise; who neither inclines to the right hand of prejudice nor to the left hand of wilfulness; who is open to the reception of all truth; who is

> " Strong without rage,
> Without o'erflowing, full. "

Rare indeed! How preposterous, then, to expect organizations to be always led by such men. No! no! we must continually act with the fanatics for good, or the fanatics for evil; for temperance, or against it. And the appeal then wisely was to be right on that grand issue, no matter who were for or who against.

Mr. President, another of the well-remembered facts is the long days of labor. In the summer time the factory bell rang in at five in the morning, and out at seven and one-half in the evening; one half-hour being given to breakfast, and another half-hour to dinner. During the winter it was rung later in the morning and later at night, the number of hours not being lessened. In other factory villages I have heard of, more hours were required and given. On the farms, in the shops of carpenters, blacksmiths, and all other trades I knew any thing of, no given number of hours were recognized as a day's work. The right of every human being to be protected by law against the unreasonable demands of employers, and the fact, which later observations have demonstrated, that more work is usually done in the shorter time, were unrecognized, if not unknown. Inventions since that time have also powerfully aided discussion in awakening the thought of the civilized world, from which has come the legislation here and in Europe on this subject. I hail it, as I pass, with devout thankfulness and hope.

Wednesday was a memorable day then, Mr. President, because it brought us the " Massachusetts Spy." Worcester had no daily paper, nor was a daily paper taken in the east village. One semi-weekly paper, the " Courier " from Boston, had one subscriber. When I was in the post-office in the centre of the town, in 1832, only four dailies were taken. They were all from Boston, and arrived the day after their date. Perhaps no one product of human skill and thought more conclusively shows the quickened intelligence and larger activities of the present, as compared with the past, than the newspaper. Of course the telegraph, the wonder of wonders, has done much in effecting this change ; but the extent of it, and the power of the press as one of its results, are among the many memorable things of our time. Last year, let us remind ourselves, we read of the battles of the Franco-German war before their smoke had passed away. The Louvre and the Hôtel de Ville were yet burning as we read the astounding news. Forty years ago, no miracle would have been more marvellous than this ! Contrast these with the declaration of war against Turkey, made at St. Petersburg, April 26, 1828, and which was published in the Boston papers June 18, fifty-three days afterwards. The bursting of the Thames into Brunel's Tunnel occurred May 17, 1827 ; and the account of it appeared in the Boston papers of June 30, *forty-four days afterwards*.

I turn now, Mr. President and friends, to a few of the men whom I most distinctly call to mind. One of great age was

Mr. Benjamin Watson, many of whose descendants are before me. He went about in his "one-hoss shay." He always sat in the pulpit, because he could there hear best the public service. Over these bleak hills he came in all seasons. I was a boy, but the impression he made on my mind of a saintly man yet remains. When I have seen in certain pictures venerable and exultant faces, waiting for the summons to depart hence, they have brought to my mind that humble and reverent listener.

Another was Mr. Solomon Parsons. He was in the battle of Monmouth, and told often in my hearing of the oppressive heat of that day, and of the wounds and sufferings he passed through, which had disabled him for life; but I remember most distinctly of all his account of General Washington. My friend, Hon. W. Flint, who has just sat down, told us he remembered his death. This man had often *seen* him, had fought under him, and spoke in such terms of him as one might fitly use of a being from another and brighter sphere.

One whom I need not name was a militia " Captain," — the first I had ever seen. He would sit in " that " store and tell how " we had whipped the Britishers," and " how we always should whip them." They were, indeed, a very contemptible foe. Now you will readily believe a good deal of what he said was new to me. He told *the other side* of the oft-repeated story. I was no little indignant. Often he seemed to me to impersonate Mars. Yet a later experience has shown that the captain in real war may give a different lesson. Did you not see how the sentiments of peace were applauded to the echo lately in Boston, when the war-scarred veterans of the Army of the Potomac were in council? And have you not also been gladdened by the sight of our greatest leader in the recent war — he who received Lee's sword at Appomattox — taking the initiative in the Treaty of Washington? So that the grandest title of all shall be his, great as were those which went before; the divinest of all benedictions: " Blessed are the peacemakers, for they shall be called the children of God." And to-day we all see, behind the dark visage of that brave warrior of ours, a genuine love of his country.

Dr. Austin Flint has been referred to, who was known so well as the "Old Doctor." No boy of my time will forget him. His grasp was like that of a vice, and he had great joy in giving us a welcome by hand-shaking. It showed no want of respect when we sometimes went out of our way to avoid his all too affectionate greeting. And what a loyal, firm, cheerful, trusty citizen he was! Towns and States and Kingdoms, under God, rest upon such men, and rest securely. This town was fortunate in having some men of great nobility of character, of which class Dr. Flint may stand as a type.

And there was a " Young Doctor ; " a true son of the old. " Doctor Ned," we then called him. There he sits ; but he does not now rank among the young men, nor do we now address him by his given name. The truth requires me to say that, as boys, we had mingled feelings towards him professionally ; but it may be some satisfaction to him to know that some of us have since gone farther and fared worse.

Mr. President, one of the events of each day in that former time, as *you* well remember, was the passing of the stages to and from Springfield and Albany. How we all stopped to watch them as long as they were in sight! and well we might ; for they were the product of large and long experience ; of great capital, judged by the standard of that day, and met and were themselves the evidence of the increasing intercourse among men. Here the stage is not quite among the things of the past, and some people are glad of it. They don't like changes, and they don't want railroads. A few weeks ago an Indian chief from the far West was in Boston. His name was " Stone Calf," and he said, " Save *us* from railroads ; " " Don't have them built through our territory ; " " They bring there bad men ; " " *Railroad men are bad men*." I fear he spoke from a bitter experience, and it was reason enough for him. I was asked to say something on railroads. It is plain that you cannot compete with other communities, on equal terms, in any branch of industry, while you are without one. It is the fact which explains your slow growth. To be without a railroad, to use an expressive phrase, "is to be out in the cold." Your young blood and enterprise go elsewhere, and will more and more; your wealth will slowly follow. You cannot stand still; you must feel the throb of a growing and expanding life in your material interests, or that torpidity which is the sure symptom of decay. Allow me to say, friends, you are abundantly able to supply this want, and the expenditure would repay your community many fold. I think, too, you will have to depend upon yourselves for it.

There are two reasons why you are not likely to get a railroad in any other way.

1st. Branch roads have not generally been found profitable, and stockholders don't expect their Directors to do what will not pay dividends.

2d. The managers of existing lines have great outlays before them to keep abreast of their urgent needs. Take, for illustration, the Boston and Albany. It ought to have a great passenger station in Boston on the scale of some of the magnificent London stations. It is to have a great one in Worcester in due time. It needs, and is building and buying more and more cars, for its urgent necessities. It is introducing steel rails; laying new tracks; straightening its curves; increasing the number and quality of its trains. And to do all these things, many hundreds of thousands of dollars are, or will be required. I respectfully submit, then, that there is no just ground of complaint, if the Boston and Albany will not build your road.

Of course, Mr. President, a road may be built by, and be profitable to, a town, although it may never pay a dividend. Am I asked how to proceed? Ascertain the best points of connection and the best routes. Look it through thoroughly. Then the question of gauge must have careful attention. If the common one of 4 feet $8\frac{1}{2}$ inches is chosen because of its manifest advantages in enabling the rolling-stock of other roads to pass over it; in saving the breaking of bulk, and in enabling you to make better terms with the trunk line with which you would connect, build one of that gauge and according to your means, having regard mainly to safety.

Consider, however, the claims of the narrow gauge, which means one between 2 feet and 3 feet 6 inches. For branch lines, or for main lines in mountainous districts, it is received with deserved favor. Last summer I went out of my way to North Wales, between one and two hundred miles, to see the Festiniog railway, pronounced, truly, the most wonderful road in the world. Its gauge is 23 inches. It is about 13 miles long,. and climbs up 700 feet among the Welsh hills to bring slate to the coast at Portmadoc. It has been the most profitable one in Great Britain. Its dividends have averaged 12½ per cent upon its total cost, after all its changes from horse to steam. I rode upon it at a speed of not less than twenty-five miles an hour. The best engineers said before parliamentary commissioners it was too narrow for steam to be used upon it with safety, and they thought it impracticable ; and but one locomotive firm, the Messrs. England, of Hatcham, would undertake it. But the impossible was accomplished. Its speed was restricted to twelve miles, on the ground again of safety, but experience showed this was a mistake ; and it is now unrestricted. With its Fairlie engines, which have proved very successful, its capacity has been greatly enlarged. Mr. Spooner, its engineer, who has had more experience with the narrow gauge than any other man living of his profession, advises a gauge of 2 feet and 6 inches. It is his opinion that even the business of the London and North-western might be done upon it.

In the early part of last year a body of engineers and commissioners of several foreign governments, all of the highest character, visited this road, and, after careful observations agreed in opinion " that the common gauge is far beyond ordinary requirements." Captain Tyler, government inspector of the English railways, has said that a system of narrow-gauge lines would cost only two-thirds as much, and be maintained at three-fourths of the expense of those in general use.

But how came this " battle of the gauges " ? Tracks were used, as you know, in the coal-mines, on which cars were pushed by hand. Afterwards these tracks were extended outside of the mines, and drawn by horses. No one knows when, or why, or by whom, it was decided that the first wooden tracks should be 4 feet 8½ inches wide. It was enough that they answered their purpose. When, however, Stephenson made his locomotive for the Liverpool and Manchester road, the question of gauge seems not to have had much attention. That of the mines was adopted, as of course; and that decision, as we now see, settled the question for nearly all the great lines since constructed. Afterwards Mr. Brunel took the ground it was too narrow for speed, comfort, and safety; and the Great Western, of England, was built with 7-ft. gauge. On this side we had the Erie, of 6 feet; the Ohio and Mississippi, the same; the Great Western and Grand Trunk, of Canada, $5\frac{1}{2}$ feet. The decision has been made to change the Great Western, of England, to the 4 feet $8\frac{1}{2}$ inch gauge; the Ohio and Mississippi has been changed already, and the Great Western, of Canada, has a third rail, giving it the same gauge. And now, Mr. President, the battle continues; but the position of the parties has changed. It is no longer between the 4 feet $8\frac{1}{2}$ inches and the wider, be it 5, or 6, or 7 feet. In that contest the narrower is master of the field, to find itself on the defensive, and assailed by the same arguments its friends so successfully urged against its rivals.

But my toast speaks of an old Leicester; and, in conclusion, let me say a few words about the Leicester beyond the sea. It is a city of some 90,000, and is known, wherever stockings are worn, for its hosiery trade. One account I have seen states the number engaged in it there at 60,000. Tradition dates the settlement of the city as far back as 800 years before the Christian era, when a King Lear lived there. Shakspeare received from it the chief incidents of the tragedy of that name, varying, however, in this, that the old chronicler had the abused king and Cordelia restored to their rightful authority. It was near Leicester that Richard III. was killed, and there he was buried, giving the great dramatist another subject to make as immortal as our English speech. Cardinal Wolsey died in its Abbey with the pathetic words, —

> " Had I but served my God with half the zeal
> I served my king, he would not in mine age
> Have left me naked to mine enemies."

It has parts of the old wall behind which it withstood sieges of Cromwell and Rupert. To the antiquarian there are Roman, Danish, and Saxon memorials, of which time will not allow me to speak. It has a Castle in which courts of justice have been held for five hundred years. A house is shown where both Bunyan and Wesley preached. Wycliffe is believed to have spoken in St. Mary's, and Milman tells us the city was full of his followers. It has old churches, — St. Margaret's is one of them, — which Saxon and Norman helped to build, and whose roofs have heard the prayers of many centuries. The chapel is shown where the noble missionary Carey once labored, and in which, also, Robert Hall delivered sermons which have gone wherever our language is spoken. De Montford, one of its Earls, called the Oxford Parliament in which representatives of boroughs had seats, and from which dates the House of Commons. His statue, and that of other benefactors of the town, adorn a handsome modern memorial structure, in one of its squares, known as the " clock-tower." And now, friends, as we have with that *really* old city, a common name, faith, speech, and literature, ought they not to awaken a common interest in each other's history, past and future? I think so. And to that end your excellent free public library, it is hoped, will soon be enriched with Nicholl's " History of Leicester and Leicestershire," a work full of local details, and illustrated with pictures of churches, castles, abbeys, Roman remains, and private residences. To the Literary and Philosophical Society of that city will be sent Washburn's History of our Leicester, together with such other publications as may interest an inquirer there who may desire to know what the Leicester men and women of this new world have thought and done.

With profound thanks for your close attention, I close with this sentiment : —

" *The Leicester of* '71. Too high for a railroad, it has been said; too low to be contented without one. A liberal public spirit, courage, and the NARROW GAUGE are the reconcilers by which its valleys may be exalted, its rough places made smooth, and the locomotive be brought to the ' Hill.' "

3. " *The City of Worcester.* While pure water bears health to her homes, she cannot forget its source in the green hills of Leicester. The current of her busy life is strengthened by our sons and daughters ; and she honors us by choosing for her chief magistrate an Earle of Leicester."

Hon. EDWARD EARLE, Mayor of Worcester, was introduced to respond, which he did, as follows : —

MR. PRESIDENT, — It does me good to look over an audience like this, and feel that I hold such a connection as this occasion denotes with so much intelligence and worth as is here repre- sented. I was invited to be present at this time and respond to the sentiment just read by the Toast-master ; and feeling that if I was titled by Worcester I could not do her justice without a few words in reply, but hearing five minutes was the time not to be exceeded, concluded as much less as was convenient might be chosen, and prepared a short set speech, which I now give you.

My few months' study in yonder academy did not embrace rhetoric, neither did our *alma mater* endow all her sons with the gift of oratory, like the one we have listened to with so much interest this forenoon. But of the city of my adoption I feel a just sense of pride in saying she ever stands ready to accord to all her neighbors full credit for all these good things. And who can say she has not laid some pipes and pulled many wires for Leicester ? Her bulwarks are her shops of industry and her temples of education. Her palaces are the homes of their directors ; her people proclaim with open arms, Come one, come all ; all may come that will come.

Now, my friends, the five minutes, and the three times five, which one if not both of those who preceded me have occupied, seems to give me liberty to say a few words in regard to my position. Till within a little more than two years past my life had been an active, practical one, so much so that I felt my time had come for some change ; and with a view to devote much of my future to charitable, benevolent, and patriotic pur- poses, I closed my most active business connections, and had truly enjoyed the benefit and comfort of the change. Last autumn I was called upon to spend three months out amongst the Indians in connection with the measures being carried on by Friends, under the peace policy of President Grant. On my return the first of the year, the city of Worcester had not forgotten to mourn for him who had so long and so faithfully served them as their chief magistrate. He had been taken from them by a sudden and unlooked-for death in my absence, and they were now to look for a new man, and soon approached me. I could not listen to it at all for a time, and resisted as long as I honorably could, but to no purpose. They overpowered me, and bestowed upon me what they termed an honor (I have often thought they must have been hard pushed for a candidate) ; as the world goes it is esteemed an honor, and it was honorable both to Leicester and Worcester, in one point, for the present incumbent was elected really as a temperance man, — which is the general character of Leicester men. Were I to take myself back in memory fifty years, I could talk in a broken way for a long time ; but fearing I might stand in the way of others and weary you, I will now close, feeling that this day is one that all of us must remember with much joy.

4. " *Spencer.* Our eldest daughter, — child of our youth. Though she has far outgrown her parent, we glory in her enterprise, industry. and wealth. Her children are as welcome as our own."

EMERSON STONE, Esq., responded. He related the difficulties experienced in procuring the act of incorporation for Spencer in 1742, twenty-one years after the incorporation of Leicester, at which time it passed the General Court, but was vetoed by Governor Shirley ; seven years later it was again attempted, and again vetoed ; but in 1753, an act of incorporation was granted, and the town was named Spencer, in honor of Governor Spencer Phips. He spoke of the years of toil and hardship experienced by the settlers after they set up in a town by themselves, until, after thirty-three years of uncertainty and homesickness, they had been smiled upon by prosperity at every decade, and from five houses the number had grown to six hundred, with nine boot shops, four woollen mills, two wire mills, and a population of four thousand. He added that if Spencer continued to prosper, she might yet be able to take charge of her mother town of Leicester, like a dutiful and affectionate child ; and then, perhaps, further prosperity would enable her to take charge of Worcester, which city would then be able to vote " No " on the beer question.

5. " *Paxton*. A child that has inherited the quiet, easy disposition of its parent. Unambitious of wealth or fame, her ways are pleasantness, and her paths are peace."

H. W. Hubbard, Esq., responded as follows : —

Paxton is pleased to be recognized by old Leicester on this glorious Fourth of July. She has not increased in population as some of the other daughters : cannot show such mammoth warehouses and gigantic manufacturing establishments ; but she hopes to gladden the old mother's heart by that inward purity and grace that is so becoming to little people and towns of the size of Paxton ; she is young, and few in years, — being only about one hundred years old or so, — while Leicester is one hundred and fifty.

> Oh ! strong may be Paxton in the power of loveliness and youth,
> And *rich* in her hearts' treasured dower of strong, unchanging truth.

6. "*Auburn*. The only portion of our original territory which can be described as a ' village of the plain.' May it more and more entitle itself to that other appellation which Goldsmith gave its prototype, and all men confess it to be the ' loveliest,' as it is the youngest of the family."

John Mellish, Esq., responded.

Mr. President, Ladies and Gentlemen, — After what we have heard from the distinguished and learned gentlemen who have so fully furnished the intellect with its treat, nothing remains but to respond as I may, in few words, to the sentiment which embraces the name of the town which I have adopted as my home.

By the act of incorporation of the town of Ward, Leicester lost its south-easterly corner, in form approximating that of an equilateral triangle, and containing about 2,500 acres. Worcester contributed about 2,200 acres ; and the rest of the town was taken from the towns of Sutton and Oxford, and from an unincorporated tract of land called the "Oxford North Gore." It was named in honor of Major-General Artemas Ward, of Shrewsbury.

In 1837, the name of the town was changed from Ward to Auburn, not, as some have seemed to suppose, for the reason that the latter is the more poetic name or more euphonious word, but mainly because the name of the town of Ware so nearly resembled that of Ward, when not carefully written, as to cause provoking delays in letters arriving at their intended destination.

The sentiment designates Auburn as the "village of the plain," for the reason, it may be, that the eminence on which it is situated is less in its altitude than is the "hill" on which this beautiful village of Leicester is built; or from the idea associated with the village called its prototype, referred to in the sentiment.

But let me say of Auburn, It is a place where "industrious habits reign;" hence it is a place of thrift; and here, if anywhere, it is that the poet's idea of the "golden mean" is realized; where none

> "Feel the wants that pinch the poor,
> Nor plagues that haunt the rich man's door."

Auburn is a peaceful town; so that no pettifogger would be able to incite litigation sufficient to furnish him the most meagre support.

It is also a healthy town; so that a physician, however skilful, must to a great degree rely for support on such practice as may be obtained outside of its limits.

Auburn has also a healthful regard for moral and religious principle; consequently its inhabitants, in goodly numbers, obey the summons of the "church-going bell."

Some interesting facts pertaining to the history of the town, or anecdotes of its people of by-gone generations, might here be related; but I refrain from trespassing on your time for that purpose, and only ask, Mr. President, permission as an old man to offer a single piece of advice to such of the young in this great company as enjoy the perusal of books which

shall at once afford amusement, entertainment, and instruction.
I say, let them for a time give the go-by to the newest novels,
and rather obtain and read the " Historical Sketches of the
Town of Leicester," by Emory Washburn.

I will close by giving you —

" *The Towns of Leicester, Spencer, Paxton, and Auburn.* May their
prosperity be secured for the future by their continuing their habits of industry, and their regard for moral and religious principle."

7. " *Our Soldiers in the late War.* We delight to cherish the memory
of their deeds, with those of their Revolutionary sires. May their example
ever inspire their countrymen in the hour of peril; may they live well-
rounded lives, as happy in the future as they have been glorious in the past,
and find in the honor and prosperity of their country their highest reward."

Lieutenant-Colonel J. A. Titus, of Worcester, responded as
follows : —

Mr. President, — It is not my purpose to pronounce an
eulogy on the conduct of your brave citizen-soldiers. That
duty properly belongs to others who surveyed the field with
more disinterested thought and observation.

But I may be indulged for a moment in an effort to uphold
the patriotic rectitude which summoned these men to the contest when the country whose birth we celebrate was threatened
by its disorganizing foes. That hour, indeed, tried men's souls ;
ignorance of duty then bespoke a nerveless and sickly ambition, beautiful in the serene atmosphere of peace, but helpless
and useless in the moment of exigency.

Not such, however, was the spirit which animated the breasts
of the noble men who represented the ancient town of Leicester in the late war. They responded to a sublime principle
of true patriotism, and offered their services on every field.

The detached records kept by the various men who served in
separate organizations, and on widely separate fields, disclose
the interesting and important fact that in nearly every important campaign of the war, and in most of its principal battles,
old Leicester was represented by some brave son.

This fact, with its details, forms the nucleus of a luminous chapter in the history of the Leicester of to-day ; and the materials should be at once intrusted to the hands of a faithful and discerning historian.

The veterans of to-day, with a proud conception of the duty done and of the institutions perpetuated by their efforts, assemble here to share with you the abundant fruition of their labors : they boast of no inborn inspiration to noble and patriotic deeds and sufferings, but fully attribute to their country, and their country's religion and law, the credit of educating them to the rational defence of civil liberty.

Those of us who bore a humble part in the war gladly recognize, in the age in which we live, the courage to do and dare which was so illustrious in our Revolutionary fathers. The iron blood matured in their veins by frequent conflict with injustice, has not turned to water in its transmission to us through three generations of their successors ; their motives, their principles, their fidelity and resolution, have been faithfully reflected in the conduct of their children.

They planted seed whose product has enriched the soil that nourished it. To us has fallen the duty of preserving this rich patrimony from unskilful and thriftless management.

The present comes to us laden with weighty responsibilities and trusts : with these responsibilities properly performed, and these trusts faithfully discharged, the future will be safe. The history of the past is sealed, but not without its testimony to the brave and true. The names of the dead shall be the choicests relics of the household shrine. Their memories shall gather deeper verdure and fresher fragrance as time glides on. Heaven grant that the living, with their enviable and glorious experience, with their recollection of the past fraught with danger to freedom, and their renown resting on their heads, may, by a strict adherence to truth, transmit the legacy of their fathers to worthy sons, having enriched the bequest with all the embellishments of wisdom, and the achievements of progress !

Fellow-soldiers ! Fame has bestowed on you her richest praise. Our flag, unsullied, waving serenely over our country and her commerce ; our laws, assuring justice and equality to every son of Adam; our institutions of learning, scattering their treasures among all classes of our busy population, — these and the thousand other blessings clustering about our government, all saved by your efforts, shall, by their beneficence at home and their power abroad, perpetually repeat, through coming generations, the encomium which is ever the greatest reward of the sincere and faithful citizen.

A choir of singers, on a raised platform at the west end of the tent, here sang the "Star-spangled Banner," accompanied by a piano and several band pieces, with fine effect.

8. "*The Orator of the Day.* A son of Leicester, who, in the Legislature, at the bar, on the bench, in the chair of the chief magistrate, and in that of a professor of Harvard University, has reflected honor upon the place of his birth. We rejoice that his fondest memories linger here, and that through his living efforts our local history has been preserved to posterity."

Mr. WASHBURN, in response, said he had already taxed the indulgence of his friends too severely that day, to be willing to trespass upon their attention again, if the sentiment had not made certain personal allusions, which ought not to pass unnoticed. His fondest memories were, indeed, connected with this spot, because they were associated with the scenes of his childhood, and the hopes of his early manhood. Every object around him on which his eye rested had a story to tell of happy hours spent here, and brought back the recollection of friends whose kindness he could never forget. He would not have referred to the marks of public favor which he had shared, to which allusion had been made, if it had not been to acknowledge, as he desired to do, how much of whatever of success he had enjoyed in life he owed to the aid and encouragement which he received from friends here in his early life. They had taken him by the hand and helped him on his way, and had been willing to overlook the follies and mistakes of his youth, while they cheered him in his efforts with words of hope and encouragement. But above all he ought to acknowledge that he owed whatever he had achieved to one whose memory would ever be sacred in his thoughts. They all knew that by

the early death of a father, he had been left an orphan boy,
dependent alone upon the kindness of a mother for his support,
and upon her counsels for guidance and direction in his childhood, and for whatever aid or patronage he had received in
fitting him to start in life. And it was to her influence and
example that he was indebted for whatever claims he might
have been supposed to have evinced for the favor with which
he had been regarded.

And in paying this humble tribute to his own mother, he
was but doing that justice which was due to the mothers as a
class, who, in his early days, were emulating the example of
those who had illustrated the noble sphere of woman, by inspiring the traits of character in this community which had
honorably distinguished the town in its earlier history. The
proprieties of the occasion would not admit of calling these by
name, and he must content himself with offering as a sentiment, —

" *The Memory of our Mothers.* Their influence sanctified and their wisdom
helped to form the policy and opinions which in times past have made Leicester honored among her sister communities."

9. " *The Clergy.* New England owes much of her greatness to their
liberal and scholarly Christian spirit; and Leicester, on this anniversary,
gratefully recognizes her indebtedness to her own ministry, whose interest
is manifest in her character and in all her best institutions."

JOSEPH L. PARTRIDGE, Esq., responded to this by reading the
following letter from Dr. NELSON, whose age forbade his response in person: —

FELLOW-TOWNSMEN AND FRIENDS, — Leicester has been settled as a town one hundred and fifty years. Ten years more
than half of this whole period I have lived in the world; and
nine years more than one-third of it I have been an inhabitant
of the town.

The first time I saw Leicester, in about 1800, I rode on
horseback from Worcester behind my uncle, who was then at-
tending the Academy. I went into the Academy building with
him, which was long and shapeless in its form, and situated

quite down to the road. It was interesting to me, as Leicester Academy was then famous, not only in the county, but throughout the Commonwealth. Besides, the building, as I understood, had been the trading-house of a rich company of Jews during the Revolutionary war, of which I had heard marvellous stories.

In 1812, I began my permanent residence in Leicester; and now the memories, the associations, and the attachments of all but sixty years from that date cause me to feel, as it were, fused into it, and to become almost a native. It is indeed a trial that age and weakness must prevent my being present with the *family* gathering to-day, if only as a specimen of its antiquity. Much more I regret it, as these infirmities must prevent my expressing by the living voice the many good things I would be glad to say of the old homestead.

Certainly it would give me pleasure to call attention to a few of the interesting occurrences and changes that have taken place during the long time of my residence in the town. But this, if it were otherwise desirable, is rendered unnecessary by the fact that the Orator of the day, always interested in his native town, and always devoted to its honor and welfare, has gone side by side with me in his observations, and put on record more of the history of Leicester than I could have gathered from the failing storehouse of my memory. But the old man and the scarcely less aged companion and fellow-pilgrim of his long and favored life can and do unitedly send their cordial greetings to Leicester's gathered sons and daughters with their friends and guests. May Heaven's choicest blessings rest on them, and the coming generations that may dwell in these valleys, or that may emigrate from them!

The PRESIDENT then introduced Rev. A. C. DENISON, of Middlefield, Ct., who was settled in Leicester, as the first colleague of the Rev. Dr. Nelson, in 1851, and was for five years the much-loved junior pastor of the original society in that place.

Mr. DENISON said: —

MR. PRESIDENT, — With great satisfaction has one of the wandering prodigals to whom you have referred, accepted the invitation to return to-day to this paternal board. But not with equal satisfaction can he respond to the call with which he has been so unexpectedly honored, of contributing to this entertainment. For after that feast of reason (and turkey) and flow of soul (and the cup which cheers but not inebriates) with which we have been so sumptuously regaled, he may well fear that the few crumbs which he may bring will be stale and insipid enough. There are a thousand tongues here to-day to which he would much rather listen than to his own; and this shall soon be silent, that those may be the sooner and the longer heard.

In behalf of my profession, however, I would gratefully acknowledge the compliment which your toast pays the clergy of New England. And having personally so little claim to the credit it ascribes to the clergy of Leicester, I may the more freely speak of those to whom such honor is justly due. I need not speak (as my heart would prompt) of the character and ability of those now on the stage of active life; for their acceptable and beneficent labors are actions which speak louder than words, and render words superfluous. Nor need I speak for those so abundantly able to speak for themselves, to whose *dissent* I cheerfully accord my *assent*, and whose names and memory Leicester will never cease to cherish. But, on such an occasion as this, we surely cannot forget one who has been so long and so closely identified with all the interests of this town, and who is himself so prominent a part of its history for about two-fifths of the entire period of its corporate existence. It were well worth the journey hither to see again that venerable form, and to hear a few words from the lips which have so often taught our willing ears lessons of heavenly wisdom. But, though we see him not before us here to-day, we cannot fail to see all around us the impress and reflection of his character and influence. The temporal prosperity of this community, the temperance, morality, industry, public spirit, and good order which here prevail, are the result in no small degree, as has well been said, of his teachings and example. It is a blessing which falls to the lot of few communities to enjoy so long the labors of such a man, — a blessing whose value is not easily computed; and in the present case we rejoice to say the time for justly estimating it has not yet arrived. It is to the credit of this good pastor and this good town, that each has appreciated the other so well as to live together so long and so happily.

History tells us that an ancient potentate, to commemorate his memory, caused a mountain of rock to be carved into a likeness of himself, hoping thus to perpetuate his features to the remotest time. Our venerable friend has done better than this. Not with selfish ambition or for ostentatious display, but in the earnest, quiet labors of a Christian pastor and friend, he has impressed his moral features on what is more imperishable than the mountain rock, — these thousands of loving, Christian hearts. These shall be his memorial when the mountains shall crumble, and the rocks decay, and the elements melt with fervent heat. How many of these have already gone before to welcome him to the heavenly land! How many yet on earth " rise up before the hoary head, and honor the face of the old man, and call him blessed "! How many can unite in that prayer, uttered for another in another age and tongue! —

" Serus in cœlum redeat," —
"Late may he return to heaven."

God bless the dear old pastor of this dear old First Church! May the sun of his life set in peaceful serenity, after its declining rays have long gilded, with a gentle radiance, the scenes which its mid-day beams have made so bright and fertile!

The PRESIDENT then said, — We have another member of the honored clergy among us, who belongs to a different religious denomination from that just represented, and who was for many years the loved and respected pastor of one of our churches in the village, and always a valuable member of our community, — and called on Rev. SAMUEL MAY for remarks.

Mr. MAY said: The kind and courteous introduction of our President deserves and has my warmest acknowledgment. And I wish to join, sir, in the heartiest and most unqualified manner, in the tribute of respect now paid to the clergy of this town, and of New England generally. I speak now of the regular Congregational ministry of New England for two hundred and fifty years. It is impossible to account for the confessedly high character which New England, as a whole, has borne, without giving a large and leading place to the influence of her clergy. This is recognized not less by the evil than by the good elements of American society. There are those who strive and desire to break down that influence ; but none who value intelligence, probity, high principle, and manly character are of the number. For fully two centuries the influence of the New-England ministry and pulpit overtopped all others, not excepting the press. And, that their influence was essentially good and sound, the appeal may safely be made to that rule, — the only rule I know which can justly claim the character of *infallibility*, — " Ye shall know them by their fruits." Not only theology and religion and good morals, but all the interests of good learning, of science, of popular education, depended chiefly upon them. Even the shaping of our social system, the enactment of wholesome laws, and the support of an honest and beneficent government, were for a long period almost exclusively with them.

Others have more appropriately represented to-day, than I can pretend to do, the great body of the New-England ministry. Let me, then, speak a few words for the clergy of dissent, — for the heretical clergy, as the phrase is, — for what in England is called the non-conforming ministry ; and let me put in, without vanity or boasting, a claim on their behalf for valuable services rendered to New England's best institutions and character.

It isn't well for anybody, you know, Mr. President, to have too easy a life. So, sir, if the lesser and heretical sects did no other good, they were useful, perhaps, on the principle of " the thorn in the flesh," in stirring up their orthodox brethren to more vigorous efforts for the faith committed to their charge. The heretics were doubtless not untruly accounted troublers of the New-England Israel ; but they also afforded favorable subjects for the spiritual doctors to exercise their dissecting skill upon, and so kept those gentlemen in good dialectic and rhetorical practice, and their instruments from getting dull and rusty; and it must be confessed that the latter were not backward in administering some very vigorous treatment to such as came in their way.

But seriously, sir, the influence of *dissent*, in a moral and religious sense, is an important one, and not to be lightly esteemed.

What, sir, is the great Protestant body, the world over, to which nearly every one of us present belongs, but a dissenting body? a forsaker of the One only Apostolic and Catholic Church, as it calls itself. Who were the Puritans, the very fathers and founders of this New England of ours, but seceders from the established Church of their country, disturbers of the English Israel, leaving the long-trodden ways of their fathers, and compelled to fly, for conscience' sake, from their homes and native land, under pains and penalties, and in peril of their lives? To-day we all honor them, and deem our descent from them our highest honor, and the heritage they left us our best possession. Yet in their day they were accounted pestilent fellows, and old England thought herself a great gainer in being well rid of them.

Sir, but for dissent, but for that spirit which asserts its freedom against all ecclesiastical as well as kingly authority, our New England had never been; and whatever she has contributed to the good of our country and the world would have been lost. That spirit agitates and purifies the world's moral atmosphere. When guided by a sense of duty and allegiance to truth, it is the mightiest power for reform and re-creation that the world can know. It is the divinity itself stirring within the soul, contending sharply and vehemently sometimes, yet striving for the " more light to break forth from God's word," and giving strength to rise above persecution, and hardship and dangers, and death even. By its means, too, we get that unity in diversity which St. Paul so eloquently describes when he speaks of " differences of administration," of " diversities of operation," but " the same spirit, the same God, working all in all."

On this theme it were easy and pleasant to enlarge, but the time does not allow, and I forbear.

We all recognize to-day the high character and valuable services of the New-England clergy. Let us also willingly and even gladly honor the principle of dissent; for of that principle we and our fathers all were born. Let us not fear to follow the motions and leadings of the soul within us. Let us encourage the search for all truth, and make it fearless, while we keep it reverent and modest. And let us willingly believe that, " after the way some call heresy," men may truly " worship the God of our fathers."

So to-day, sir, we cheerfully recognize the good work done for Leicester and for all New England by her clergy of every name. Most of all must we honor them, when above all forms they prefer the life and freedom of the human soul; when their service is rendered " in newness of the spirit, and not in the oldness of the letter; " when, with a manly and far-reaching vision, they subordinate all ecclesiastical rules and arrangements to the freedom and growth of God's children upon the earth.

Nor can we forget, sir, on this historical occasion, that portion of the people of Leicester, of whom scarcely more than a single member now remains, who accepted no clergy, recognized no special ministry, — the so-called " Friends." Once they were numerous here, and that within the recollection of most of this audience. But now their house of meeting and worship stands silent in yonder woods, and the venerable forms of men and women which once gave such a dignity and charm to those precincts lie around it in many unnamed graves. We do not, and we cannot, forget their worth, the influence of their peculiar spirit, the lessons of integrity they taught here, the courtesy and good-will of their simple manners.

Therefore we rejoice to-day in all these memories, in all that God has done for us and for our fathers. We recognize, joyfully, his providence upholding all, leading us all, saving our nation in many a fearful peril, even with a mighty hand and an outstretched arm. We gratefully bless him for the peace, prosperity, and ample field of progress in knowledge and in justice, which he grants us; and reverently say, May God be with us and our children, as he was with our fathers!

10. "*Leicester Academy*. Coeval in its origin with the American Republic, and like it still flourishing in vigorous and useful life, its benign influences have been felt for nearly a century in every part of the land. May it remain to tell future generations of the wisdom and liberality of its founders."

JOSEPH L. PARTRIDGE, Esq., of Lawrence, responded, in the absence of Judge CHAPIN, as follows: —

MR. PRESIDENT, — I do exceedingly regret, and I know that this large company must much more regret, that the gentleman who was expected to respond to this sentiment fails to do so.

It certainly is appropriate, on this day of so many hallowed and happy reminiscences to this assembly, that LEICESTER ACADEMY should receive honorable mention.

In the failure to which I have alluded, you may perhaps, sir, have been led to call upon me for a response, by the fact that I am now the oldest surviving principal preceptor of the institution. Unexpectedly called upon, as I am, my remarks will have one element which I know will be acceptable at this late hour, — they will be *brief*.

This Academy, chartered in 1783, — the third in the State, — was early among the leading influences in shaping the civil and religious institutions of the Commonwealth. Highly creditable, too, has been her standing among scientific and literary institutions, as they have multiplied from that period to the present.

In her material embodiment here, she stands looking down upon her sons and daughters with silent approval, in the midst of these festivities. But her spirit pervades the continent.

We have had portrayed to us, by the Orator of the day, the origin and the progress, from her infancy, of this among the earliest townships of the colony, the influence of her civilians in the legislative councils, and the prowess of her soldiers on numerous battle-fields, early and recent, which established and have secured the nation's liberties. We point with pride to this Academy as among the chief sources of this influence.

We have been reminded, too, how widely scattered, from North to South, and from the Atlantic to the Pacific, are the sons and daughters of Leicester, and of their honorable position wherever located.

In a word, then, sir, as the most fitting response that can be made to the sentiment you propose to " Leicester Academy," I appeal to the *high standing in intelligence and virtue* of the successive generations whose characters have been formed under the shadow of this institution, both those who have " tarried by the stuff," and those who, in person, have disseminated this influence to the boundaries of the nation.

The band was called upon to play at this point, the regular toasts having been disposed of; and voluntary sentiments and speaking were called for.

The PRESIDENT remarked that, in the address of this forenoon, allusion had been made to the resistance offered to the passage of the Sixth Regiment of Massachusetts Volunteers through the streets of Baltimore in 1861, and said that he saw before him an honored son of Leicester who commanded that regiment at the time, and could tell us all about it.

He introduced General EDWARD F. JONES, of Binghampton, N. Y., who responded as follows : —

MR. PRESIDENT AND FRIENDS OF MY BOYHOOD, — I came here to-day to mingle my greetings with yours, not expecting to speak ; but I should be sadly wanting in courtesy, did I not at least thank you for the compliment conveyed by your call; which I heartily do. Your toast implies that you expect me to recount the scenes of the first blood of the Rebellion, when the mob attacked the Sixth Massachusetts Regiment (which I had the honor to command) on its passage through Baltimore, on the 19th of April, 1861. Those scenes, long since passed, furnish a prominent page in the history of our country; and, being so familiar to all, need not be further adverted to here, except to say that the sons of Leicester did not disgrace their old mother on that occasion, nor in the hundreds that followed, in which they were engaged with either the army or the navy. "Out of the fulness of the heart the mouth speaketh." How can I, on such an occasion as this, think, much less speak, on any subject but the scenes of my childhood? Their memory crowds away all other subjects; and I am for the moment a boy again, and feel as if I could only with trembling lips say, —

> "You'd scarce expect one of my age
> To speak in public on the stage."

But, my friends, if I must talk to you about the army and navy, the only picture of the army that is at all fresh in my mind is that of my barefooted playfellows, who, with tin pan for a drum, wooden swords, and broomsticks for guns, made every neighborhood which we invaded uninhabitable, more from the din of our *music* than the devastation of our march; and as for the navy, none is at this moment rememberable, unless it be the two old flat-bottom boats that were on Upper Tophet Pond.

As I came into town this morning, after an absence of more than twenty-five years, I stopped for a moment at the house of the Rev. Dr. Nelson, that good old man who has been so feelingly referred to in to-day's proceedings, and who fills so large a place in the hearts of the people of Leicester. The grasp of his hand did not seem to satisfy me; and, had I followed the impulse of my heart, with bended knee would I have craved a blessing from this patriarch in Israel.

Passing up the street, by the residence of Dr. Flint, the remembrance of an old grudge against him came fresh to my mind. I am sorry that he has left, but will appeal to your sympathies, and ask if there is not justification for a *painful* recollection of him. After suffering beyond my boyish endurance with the toothache, it was finally decided that nothing but a judicious application of cold steel could stop it. After repeated failures I finally mustered up sufficient courage to start for the doctor's; but it seemed to be a question whether I had pluck enough to last me the quarter of a mile I had to go, but got there somehow. You no doubt have heard the saying, " The sight of you is good for sore eyes; " well, the sight of the doctor cured my toothache, and I wanted to go home, but it was of no use; it was a very healthy season, and the doctor had a plenty of leisure and but few patients; he was bound to have that quarter, *the mercenary wretch;* it was finally compromised by his agreeing to give me a ninepence, and I, like a fool, sat down on the floor and trusted my head between his knees — ough — do any of you remember his old turnkey? he was a tender man, he was; and so, not to hurt my mouth with his old snag-puller, he took his red bandanna and wound around the instrument so that it filled my mouth and some to spare; and what added to the enjoyment of the occasion, as if any addition was necessary, the doctor took snuff, — bah! — and to this day I have never been able to decide which was the worst, the toothache, the snuffy handkerchief, or the pulling. Did any of you ever get as much for a ninepence?

Sitting here to-day on these hard seats brings to mind those other hard seats over there in the Academy; and, in furtherance of the illusion, there sits our old preceptor, Mr. Partridge. Whispering to a friend just now, I looked up and caught Mr. Partridge's eye: he either did not see me whispering, or thought he would overlook it for this once.

But, my friends, with all our hand-shakings and glad greetings, there is a sad side to our festivities. To those like myself who have not been here for many years, there seem many vacant places at this festive board. Many a face whose smile of welcome we expected has vanished from earthly scenes. We miss the warm hand-clasp of almost numberless expectant friends. In my first greetings this morning, I gayly asked after the absent ones, but the answer, DEAD, shocked and startled me by its frequency; so I gladly welcomed those I saw, and asked not for the absent, for 'tis pleasanter that one's friends should live in memory than to know that they are dead.

Again thanking you for your kindly welcome, I bid you good-by, hoping that you will not let many years pass before you bid your sons and daughters home again.

The PRESIDENT read the following volunteer sentiment: —

" Hon. Nathan Sargent. An honored descendant of a patriotic ancestor of the same name, who has exhibited in the civil service of the government the sterling honesty and integrity of character he inherited from his ancestors."

To which Hon. NATHAN SARGENT, of Washington, D. C., responded as follows: —

MR. PRESIDENT, — In rising to respond to the sentiment you have kindly announced, I must first express the very great pleasure it has given me to receive an invitation to be present at this celebration.

Though not one of the *sons* of Leicester, I am, at least, a *grand*son, since both of my parents were " to the manor born," and Leicester holds within her bosom all that was mortal of my grandparents, paternal and maternal, and great numbers of others of my kith and kin. Her soil is, therefore, sacred to me.

You have been pleased to remember, on this occasion, the Sargent family; and it strangely happens that I am the only representative of that family now present, bearing the Sargent name, though one of them owns and occupies the old homestead where he whose honored name I bear settled about one hundred and thirty years ago, and upon which he lived fifty-six or fifty-eight years, and his second wife, my grandmother, seventy-one years. The name of Nathan Sargent was therefore, for the period of two generations, familiar to the Leicester people, and few were more respected.

But, Mr. President, I came not to pronounce a eulogy upon my ancestors, nor to exhume them; but, representing and being expected to say something of them, though in the briefest manner, I will simply illustrate their character by one or two personal anecdotes.

And first, let me say, their characters were formed, as others are, by the times in which they lived, the general mode of thinking, the soil they tilled, and the climate by which they were surrounded. The two latter were rough and ungenial. Nothing could be obtained from the soil but by ceaseless labor;

and, during the few months of seed-time, growth, and harvest, they had to provide the necessary food and clothing for themselves and families, and sustenance for their stock during the long months and short days of snow and frost.

They had little time or money to spend in amusements or pleasure, and none to throw away upon the luxury of lawsuits. I hope the anecdote I am about to relate may be as characteristic of the good people of Leicester now as it was a hundred years ago.

One of the judges of the county court, which sat at Worcester, in conversation with Colonel Seth Washburn, asked him how it happened that there were never any suits in that court from Leicester. Colonel Washburn replied, "Because our land is poor, cold, and rocky, and we have as much as we can do to get a living off of it, and no time nor money to spend in lawsuits." But they had time and money to spend in establishing an Academy, which is a monument to their appreciation of learning, their desire to benefit their children and their children's children, and an enduring honor to the town.

Mr. President, anticipating that I might be called upon to contribute my mite to this entertainment, and expecting to tell you something about the "Sargent family" which was not familiar to you all, and which should at the same time illustrate the average character of a Leicester man a century ago, I had got together a nice string of anecdotes, set off with a few brilliant thoughts and wise reflections, which I calculated would be received with great attention, interest, and applause, amidst which I should resume my seat full of calm delight and self-appreciation. But

> "The best-laid schemes o' mice an' men
> Gang aft a-gley."

And so did mine, and that highly interesting speech I was to make here was knocked in the head; for, on looking over Washburn's "History of Leicester," I found, to my chagrin, he had written it all out there a dozen years ago.

He has told you that my grandfather, discovering that the company of "minute-men," commanded by Captain Washburn, which had halted in front of Mr. Sargent's house, on its march to Boston, were destitute of bullets, took the weights from his clock and had them run into balls, and that the company was thus supplied. Now there is no doubt of the truth of this anecdote; and I have here one of the very bullets thus cast, which was picked up on Bunker Hill twenty-odd years ago, where that company was engaged in battle. If any one doubts whether it is one of the clock-weight bullets, let him prove that it is not.

My paternal ancestor, like the Leicester people generally of olden time, had a kindly, benevolent heart hid away under a rough exterior, with a sturdiness of manner more resembling the rough climate of Leicester than that of the palm and the orange, as will be illustrated by the following anecdote, not to be found in Washburn's " History of Leicester."

There were seasons in the olden time when, owing to late or early frosts, the crops, and especially the corn crop, failed. To you, people of Leicester, it is now matter of small moment whether your corn crop is a full or a short one, because you depend mainly upon other parts of the country for your bread-stuffs, which are brought to your doors by means of cheap and rapid transportation.

Not so with our ancestors; no railroads or steamboats ena-bled them to draw supplies from distant parts; nor did those supplies then exist. They had to depend solely upon what they themselves raised; and when an early frost deprived them of their necessary supply of corn, they were reduced to great straits. During one of these seasons, Colonel Washburn came down, like the children of Israel of old, to buy corn, not of Joseph, but of Nathan, who, owning and running a mill, had corn to sell. " Have you the money to pay for it?" asked Mr. Sar-gent. " Yes," was the reply. " Then you can't have it," said Mr. Sargent. " Why not?" asked Colonel Washburn. " Be-cause you have money, and can go into some other town and buy what you need; the poor of our town have no money, and can't get it elsewhere; and my corn is for them."

Such was an old-time Leicesterian, or, in the language of the day, " a representative man," honest, kind, benevolent, consid-erate, plain-spoken.

My friend and kinsman, the Orator of the day, and the Historian of Leicester, has spoken with filial respect and affection of his mother; and has said that, if he deserved any of the honors that had been so liberally (and permit me to say *justly*) bestowed upon him by his native town and State, he owed it all to the influence of his mother.

Let me follow his example, and say that, if I am deserving of any of the kind expressions contained in the toast you have done me the honor to announce, I owe it to a mother born and reared in Leicester; a woman not unworthy of the exemplary and patriotic mothers and daughters among whom she was reared, — a pious, intelligent, loving " mother in Israel." I was reared under all those influences which formed the character of both my parents, and which have come down to us all here present from the first settlers of Leicester, our noble ancestors. What I am, therefore, I owe in a great degree to Leicester.

Mr. President, I will detain you only to express the hope that those who shall celebrate the two hundredth anniversary of the organization of this town, among whom I hope may be my grandson, Nathan Sargent, may find themselves as far in advance of us in all that contributes to the health and comfort of man, in the industrial arts, education, and general diffusion of knowledge, as the present age is in advance of those who first put the plough into the rocky hills of your now beautiful town.

I give you in conclusion, —

" *The Mothers of Leicester.* To them we owe a debt of gratitude for the moral and religious principles they instilled into the minds of those whose lives daily illustrate them at home, as well as those who have carried them to distant parts, to take root and spread abroad."

The toast —

" *Mulberry Grove, — the Home of the Friends.* Their firesides were love and affection; their *thee* and *thou*, the ever-ready welcome " —

was responded to by T. K. EARLE, Esq., of Worcester, as follows : —

As I turn back the record of the past, and live again in the "scenes of my childhood," — "the orchard, the meadow, the deep-tangled wildwood, and every loved spot that mine infancy knew," — there comes such a rush of memory, such an avalanche of thought, that the poor common words of expression can give no measure of the heart's intensity. "Mulberry Grove!" What a volume in a word! The hill of my home, the home of my boyhood, the joy of my youth, the strength of my manhood! Oh! as memory goes back to those summer Sabbath mornings, I see, in the valley of its worship, the gathering of its people in silent devotion, where in the stillness of the hour they called for the prostration of the soul before the Majesty of heaven, for the offering of spiritual sacrifices acceptable to God by Jesus Christ.

There was no architectural display, no external rites and ceremonies, no delusive charms of musical excitement, save the pine-tree's anthem, the warbling birds, and the babbling brook. These remain, all else is gone. Their sweet melody is ever sounding a requiem over the departed, and "Mulberry Grove" has ceased to be, and footsteps of angels mark the repose of its simple people.

But why look mournfully into the past? It comes not back again. Wisely improve the present: it is ours. Let us go forth to meet the shadowy future without fear and with manly hearts, for it is big with momentous events. We are struggling in the throes of a new birth: a mighty revolution is upon us.

This labor question will move the foundations of society, social and political. Very few comprehend its magnitude. Let us read aright the signs of the times, that we may carry it to its successful issue; and by the light of the glorious gospel, our wills falling in with God's, the problem shall be solved.

Mr. WASHBURN asked permission to remind the company of what he had already spoken in his address, — the sources of the growth and present prosperity of the town. It led him to recall the changes through which the productive industry of the

town had been passing within his own recollection. He re-
called an incident which served to mark some of these changes.
They were all familiar with the succession of manufacturing
establishments along the stream which flows towards the east
into the Blackstone, that are now in constant and successful
operation. But they should remember this was the result of
artificial skill and enterprise. He well recollected that, when he
was ten years old, he, in company with some mates, attempted
to " go in a-swimming " in that stream, but could not find a
spot where there was sufficient depth of water to admit of doing
it. It was upon that stream that a woollen manufactory was
commenced in 1814, and became the pioneer enterprise of all
the establishments which were now in operation in the town.
The name of the individual to which the town owes so much
ought to be gratefully remembered ; and he begged, therefore,
to offer as a sentiment, —

" *Samuel Watson*, the father and founder of the woollen-manufacturing
of Leicester. Let his name be honored, for his enterprise has blessed his
native town."

Isaac T. Hutchins, Esq., of West Killingly, Ct., who married the daughter of Samuel Watson, Esq., and who was
seated by the side of his venerable father-in-law, responded by
saying, —

Mr. President, — Although uninvited and unannounced,
and withal almost an entire stranger, I cannot keep my seat
while a father near and dear to me has been so highly complimented, as well in the address to which we have listened as
here. I was, I confess, as one born to him out of due time ; and,
what may appear anomalous, I am honored by being his oldest
as well as youngest child. I am thinking that it is about time we
dispersed ; else we may perchance, like the three disciples, desire
to make tabernacles, and remain here permanently. It has
seemed to me, while listening to the laudations of this locality
as if, through some oversight, a circuit hereabouts was omitted
in the otherwise universal apostasy. Indeed, I cannot avouch
for the truth of the assertion ; but I have often heard it said

that long ago the citizens of Massachusetts, both male and female, met and without a dissenting voice formed themselves into a mutual admiration society. I hail, sir, from the land of steady habits, — unfortunately as steady to bad ones as good; the first State in the Union and probably spot on the globe where education was made substantially free, and will probably be the last to exorcise the foul taint of slavery from its Constitution. I do not wonder, Mr. President, that you are proud of your Commonwealth, among the oldest in the sisterhood, — although I have allowed myself to speak thus lightly of her. Rev. Mr. May was truly magnanimous, as well as eminently just, in his estimate of our Puritan fathers and their stern orthodox religious faith. I felt myself personally complimented, for I claim to be a descendant of one of the passengers of the Mayflower. Mr. President, did it ever occur to you that the two greatest discoveries made in the world, during the period you to-day celebrate, were made by the two sons of Massachusetts Congregational clergymen? — the one having taught us to speak so loud as to be heard around the world, and the other having instructed us how to send messages of love, thanksgiving, and praise through the depths of the ocean, thus making "dragons and all deeps" to utter the praises of their God. Do you doubt, sir, — I do not, — that both of these were rocked to sleep in their infancy by the music of Watts's cradle hymns, and that both were in their boyhood faithfully instructed in the now nearly obsolete Assembly's Catechism.

That one of these was thus early instructed in the puritanic faith is faintly shadowed forth by his reverent repetition of a passage of Scripture, at the recent unveiling of a monument erected to his honor: "Not unto us, not unto us, but to Thy name be the praise." I will detain you only to add that while thus taking a cursory retrospect of the vast discoveries made, and the signal events which have transpired, during the last century and a half, the inquiry comes unbidden, What shall come to pass during the same period in the future? We attentively listen, and the only response which returns back to us is the faint whisper, What?

Simon P. Hastings, Esq., of Philadelphia, was then called out, who said, —

It is with mingled feelings of pain and pleasure, of joy and sadness, that a crowd of reminiscences, covering a period of more than fifty years, come rushing in upon me, in spite of myself and all I see around me. Recollections of innocency and tender childhood, of a devoted and dearly beloved mother, my father and eleven loving brothers and sisters, — eight of whom, with father and mother, have gone to their reward.

The fathers and mothers of fifty years ago, and their children who were my play and school companions, — where are they? With few exceptions, their perishable bodies lie in yonder cemeteries, mouldering and mingling with the common earth, the way of all flesh.

Forty-seven years have been numbered with the past since I, a lad of thirteen, left, with her blessing and benediction, the hospitable home of the sainted mother of the honored, beloved, and respected orator who has to-day charmed us with his eloquence ; and to-day I am permitted to return to the loved scenes of childhood with a heart overflowing with gratitude to our Heavenly Father, whose loving kindness and tender mercies have followed me all my life long. I congratulate you, my fellow-townsmen, on the success which has attended the celebration of the one hundred and fiftieth anniversary of the organization of the town of Leicester ; and I tender the Committee of Arrangements my thanks for giving me the opportunity of being present on this occasion : it has afforded enjoyment and pleasure that will go with me through the remaining days of my life.

"*Dear old Mother Leicester.* May she ever be, as to-day, by her devotion to the cause of education, by her enterprise, her industry and prosperity, a spring of joy and pride to her returning sons and daughters!"

The following sentiment was announced from Rev. James Thurston, of West Newton : —

" *The Good Town of Leicester*; one hundred and fifty years of age, her sunny hills, her shady groves, her fertile fields, her happy and cultured homes, her sons and daughters far and near. May her future prosperity be as conspicuous as her hills, as refreshing as her groves, as fertile as her fields, as lovely and attractive as her homes, as honorable to the community as her sons and daughters."

From Miss PHILENA UPHAM, Leicester : —

"When Governor Corwin, of Ohio, returned after a long absence at Washington, he thus addressed a gathering of neighbors : ' I rejoice once more to bathe in the faces of the people.' The crown and comfort of this exultant day to us is derived from our expectations fulfilled and our design accomplished. The sons and daughters of Leicester, who from time to time have taken flight, are now returned to the parent nest ; and once more, ere we wrap the drapery of our couch about us and lie down to pleasant dreams, we can ' bathe in the faces of the people ; ' once more we can greet them as we were wont to greet them in our greener years, and with doors free and open prate to them of 'ye olden time.' This occasion gives us, as Viola said, ' a very echo of the seat where love is throned.' May this festival be rosemary in our remembrance till we ' hear the rush of angel wings upon God's errand speeding'! "

From Mrs. CAROLINE H. METCALF, Worcester : —

" The memories of the fathers are the inspiration of the sons. May the spirit of our fathers be revived in their children to the latest generations."

From J. PARTRIDGE, Esq., Paxton : —

" May the policy of the government of the United States with foreign nations be the same in the future as it has been in the past, — to ask nothing but that which is right, and to submit to nothing wrong."

Rev. Mr. MAY read the beautiful lines from Dr. Holmes, as expressive and pertinent : —

" There are no times like the old times, — they shall never be forgot !
  There is no place like the old place, — keep green the dear old spot !
  There are no friends like the old friends, — may Heaven prolong their lives !
  There are no loves like our old loves, — God bless our loving wives ! "

" Yankee Doodle " and " Auld Lang Syne," by request, played with spirit and earnestness by the band, at half past five o'clock, were the last of the exercises. The success of the day was complete. The gun that awakened the good people of the town at sunrise, spoke again at sunset; and a concert by the band on the Common was the chief feature of the evening.